1960, Indonesia. The tropical paradise has suffered years of war, martial law and political upheaval which is soon to turn into economic depression and dictatorship. Nursing student Heidi West is so determined not to be offered up on a marital auction block by her mother that she accepts a post that no other student has been willing to take: a post as a surgeon's assistant off the coast of Java. The heat, the monsoons, the unrest and the isolation don't intimidate half as much as the man with whom she must live and work: The Dutch Doctor.

The Dutch Doctor

Perle Butcher Lyon

Published by Inknbeans Press

Cover: Evonne

The Dutch Doctor
© 2012 Perle Butcher Lyon
and Inknbeans Press

SBN-10: 0988667010
ISBN-13: 9780988667013

This is a work of fiction. Names, characters, places, organizations, businesses or incidents portrayed in this novel are the product of the author's imagination, used fictitiously or

Changing is hard. Not changing is harder.

Chapter One
The Decision

The air was thick and still. The only movement in the darkened peach colored house was the inexorable jerk of the minute hand on the old grandfather's clock in the sitting room and the slow swaying of a raffia fan in the kitchen. Finally, even the fan stilled. The doctor sighed and leaned forward, resting his head on his forearms. It seemed inhumane to ask a woman to come to this Asian oven, but he needed a nurse and wasn't yet liberated enough to accept a male nurse in his surgery. The only bright hope was the kind of woman willing to take an assignment such as this usually came from hardy stock and could survive, perhaps even thrive on these islands. He smiled into the cradle of his arms.

"You *do* understand you'll be living in?" The registrar's brow wrinkled up in concern.

I wrinkled my brow in response. "I'm not a home nurse," I explained politely. "I'm training to be a surgery assistant." Being a home nurse was quite probably the very last thing I wanted to do. The application had clearly stated this position was for a surgery assistant, but that wasn't why it had caught my attention. It was probably a combination of the yellowed state of the card - it had dozens of pinholes and fingerprint smears, indicating that it had been taken down, examined and replaced several times over a long period of time – and the fact that the assignment was for a position half way around the world, in Indonesia. The job description had included housing as part of the benefits, as well as a salary that was very generous for a trainee, but said nothing about 'living in'.

"Yes, I'm fully aware of your training. You're probably the only qualified applicant to get this far in the interview process." The registrar pulled out a dogeared index card from a file. It was covered in date stamps, notations in different colored inks and varying handwriting styles, indicating that many people had discussed the position, but it remained unfilled. "He's requesting a surgeon's assistant, but the facilities are somewhat limited. He practices out of his home." The registrar paused and I could see that she was putting her words together carefully. "He's a bit old fashioned. He practices the way his father did and his grandfather." She shook her head as she replaced the card. "He's been without a nurse for almost eight months, and I understand he's been contacting every nursing school here and in Europe."

"Why? His salary is generous, and his reputation appears to be excellent." I glanced at the box where she had filed the card. "Why should he be having so much difficulty getting a nurse? It doesn't make any sense." I wanted it to make sense. I wanted the assignment. If I refused it, I'd just have to go back to Savannah and wait for another one. And waiting meant pressure from all fronts to marry Jarad Frampton and become his unpaid nurse and housekeeper. I wanted more than that. I *deserved* more than that.

The registrar looked more uncomfortable than ever. "There is a lot of political unrest in the country right now," she began, at last. "Not where he is located," she added quickly, "but on the mainland and many of the larger islands." She hesitated again. "It is also very remote. There are not many distractions: no shops or restaurants or nightclubs."

"That's fine. I mean, about the nightclubs," I amended, flustered. I knew a lot of my fellow nursing students had chafed at the restrictions of a Catholic teaching hospital, but I reveled in it; the solitude, the confinement, the enforced focus on studies kept me happy and made me a better student. The restrictions also kept my mother and her influence limited to a few phone calls and one visit a month. That was the best part of all. "All right," I agreed, at last, "when would I leave?"

The relief showed in the registrar's face as she pushed forms across the desk. "Just sign these papers and we can put you on a plan to Jakarta Wednesday, if your passport is in order."

I had grown up in the sultry, swampy heat of Savannah, Georgia, but that had not prepared me for the wall of blistering humidity that swung at me like a baseball bat as I stepped off the plane in Jakarta. In moments, my pale blue gabardine suit had become a soggy second skin, and I could feel my hair lose its curl and cling stubbornly to my cheeks, brow and neck. As I stood on the tarmac, swimming in the thick air, being stared at by small, olive colored people with black hair, black eyes, and clothing that ranged from tropical whites to dark clothes and headscarves on women, my first reaction was a desire to turn around and climb back on the plane. This place, these people were so different from anything I'd ever known that even Jarad Frampton was a better proposition.

One of the men broke away from the cluster near the gate and marched right up to me. He wore faded khaki shorts that reached past his knees, and a slightly soiled white shirt with white embroidery and long sleeves, but his hair was meticulously combed and slicked down. Without a smile or a bow or any other sort of courtesy, he pointed to my bag. "Dutch doctor?" he demanded in a voice surprisingly free of the expected accent.

I shook my head, bewildered. "I'm sorry, I'm not a doctor, I'm a-"

"You want the Dutch doctor?" He made an impatient gesture with both hands. "Come, come."

I wasn't really sure I wanted a Dutch doctor, but I had been assured by the agency that I would be met at the airport and this fellow was the only one around willing to have anything to do with me, and even he was marching off without another word. I followed as quickly as the heat and the weight of my baggage would allow.

My guide appeared to be racing a clock, striding through throngs as thick as the air. He took no notice of whether or not I could keep up with him. I barely managed to follow, my eyes glued to the back of his shiny head, almost oblivious to my surroundings. I was dimly aware of flags with very militaristic symbols, and billboards and banners draped on the side of buildings featuring the face of a man. I suppose the smile was supposed to be friendly and avuncular, but magnified to the size of a tank it seemed sinister to me. There were soldiers on street corners, too. At least, I assume they were soldiers; dressed in khaki shorts and shirts with arm bands and bandoliers, side arms and expressionless faces, they watched the populace, hands behind back, but ever diligent.

My guide stopped as abruptly has he had started, some fifteen minutes later, and I found myself at a dock, surrounded by water and what I suppose were houses.

I stared at the neighborhood in horror and disgust. Before me was some sort of channel, a main waterway through a rough section of the city. The decrepit buildings were made of wood and corrugated metal and, in some cases, cardboard, and built on pilings in the water. Small boats zipped in and out amongst the rickety, sagging piers and garbage floated freely in their wake. Was this really where I had signed on to work?

One of the little boats raced across the channel and nearly rammed the wooden wharf where we stood, the engine whining and belching out fumes. Two young women, one with her head covered in a bright blue scarf, looked up at us. My guide pointed out along the channel. "Dutch doctor," he repeated.

The girls nodded knowingly and the one not on the tiller indicated that I must come down into the boat. I would have argued but my bag had already been tossed aboard. As I stepped down gingerly, trying not to breathe in the stench of the water, the man who brought me pointed at the boat. "One dollar," he said in a tone that made it very clear there would be no haggling over the fee. "U.S."

I sighed and fished a dollar out of my purse. Evidently, I was paying a dollar for the privilege of being taken to my doom. No sooner had the money left my fingers than the boat pulled away with such force that I was knocked backwards and I ended up flat on my back in a puddle of water at the bottom of the boat.

Momentarily stunned, I lay there, staring up at the sky, listening to the two women giggle. I wanted to do this, I reminded myself. I could have gone to a secular nursing school. I could have gotten a position in a hospital in Atlanta, Los Angeles, New York City, or even Savannah where all my comforts and pleasures were. But, I chose a missionary school, and a missionary assignment, because I wanted to take my skills where they were most needed – far away from my mother and Jarad Frampton. Struggling to sit up and feeling a pinch in my back, I suspected that my skills were going to be most needed right there in that little skiff.

When I finally managed to sit upright, clinging to the side of the skiff for balance, the filthy ghetto had disappeared. They were skipping along open water, hugging the coast of Java, which looked serene and green over the blue scarfed head on one of my pilots. "Excuse me, where are we-" I twisted around to look ahead and saw a horizon dotted with islands. "Oh, of course." I smiled at the two women who, up close, looked more like two little girls. The registrar had mentioned that I wouldn't be working on the mainland, but on one of the tiny islands that dotted the coastline. According to her, the doctor, two priests and I would be the only non-natives living there.

My mother had been horrified by this prospect. She was convinced that my pale skin and gold hair would make me some sort of prize among the local men. Judging from the looks from men I'd encountered since landing, I don't think my mother had anything to worry about. Most of them ignored me, and the few that did look my way looked at me in amusement and curiosity but not desire. My pale skin and gold hair just made me funny looking in their eyes.

We raced along, the little skiff bouncing hard on the water, making me clutch the side for fear that I would be tossed out. Evidently the first few islands weren't good enough for us. We hugged the coast as the water got choppy and came around a small outcrop of land which revealed the Sunda Strait between Java and Sumatra. As the strait opened into a wide bay more islands came into view. The girls chattered between themselves and aimed the boat toward the first island. It took almost an hour to reach an inlet where a dock jutted out along brilliantly white sand. A blue black mountain peak rose up out of a wreath of intense green, and a row of long, low white buildings lined the shore, with one almost comically tall, peach colored building making an exclamation point at the end.

With one girl holding the solid, white washed dock, the other girl tossed my bag up on the wooden deck and they barely gave me enough time to scramble out before they zoomed away.

To my great dismay, it wasn't any cooler on the island than it had been in the middle of Jakarta. I stood on the dock, my possessions at my feet, considering my next step (tears were my first choice, but it was too hot) when a tall, dark man in khaki shorts and a white shirt strode out of the peach colored building, his hands wound in a green cotton towel. "Are *you* the nurse?" he demanded in clipped tones, still twenty paces off.

I nodded, bending to collect my things. "Yes. Yes, I am." I stood, juggling my shoulder bag and duffel. He hadn't moved to assist me.

"Von Hollow," he said impatiently, "Doctor von Hollow. Come this way." And just like my guide at the airport, he turned with a jerk of his head and started toward the peach colored house.

Von Hollow…of course! Dutch doctor. I tried to run to keep up with him but the soft sand caught at my shoes more than the sidewalks of Jakarta did. He didn't look

Dutch. Weren't Dutch people blond with blue eyes? He had very dark skin and black hair, in fact, he reminded me of the previous guide, although his clothing was in better repair and he was very tall. From my perspective, staggering along behind him, he seemed as tall as his house.

Half way up the beach, he stopped and looked back at me. "You shouldn't run in this heat," he admonished. "It will kill you." He waited until I had slowed to an approved gait and when I got close enough, he relieved me of the duffel. "When will the rest of your things arrive?" he asked, reaching the house and nudging the bottom half of what I had always called a Dutch door open with his foot.

"This is all I brought," I said breathlessly. It was cool inside, miraculously cool. I just wanted to stand there, beside the door, and breathe in sweet, oxygen rich air.

He set my bag down beside a flight of tiled steps. "These are all your worldly possession?" he asked with an arch of one jet brow.

Distracted by the dark green walls and rows of knickknacks down the hallway it took me a moment to understand his question. "Oh, no," I assured him brushing limp curls back from my sticky face. "This is just what

I brought for the six months of my assignment."

"Six months!" He swore profusely (at least, I assumed he was swearing.) "I don't need a temporary, I need someone fulltime." He reigned in his emotions with a deep sigh. "Well, I've been without for so long, I'll take what I can get. I'm in the middle of surgery now, so go get into a uniform and we'll do the formalities later." He pointed to a door on the other side, next to the archway that led to the kitchen. "You can change in there. I hope you brought cotton uniforms. Rayon is useless in this climate." He turned on his heel and disappeared down the long, green hallway.

For once I was glad my mother was old fashioned. Rayon, she said, was cheap. A lady always wore silk. But, if one couldn't afford silk, there was no shame in wearing cotton. I picked up the bag that held my uniforms, stockings and starched caps and went into the bathroom to change out of my soggy suit and pin up my damp hair.

Knowing that he had been without a nurse for eight months, I expected to find chaos the order of the day in the office, but when I emerged from the bathroom, shielded in my brilliant whites, and went down the hall to the door where he had disappeared, I found an office so organized, a surgery so well run that it seemed impossible that he could have been operating more than fifteen minutes without the aid of a nurse.

There were two doors from the hall into the surgery. The first one went into a small, efficient office with a typewriter and six cabinets for files, a counter and a gate that opened into a waiting room decorated in blue and green and filled with patients who smiled at me and talked among themselves, pointing at me. The second door went into the examination room, which was twice the size of the office, with two exam tables and a curtain run between them for privacy. Off the examination room was a lav and a small dark room for x rays. Throughout there wasn't a speck of dust, a chart out of place, or a hint of confusion. The patients knew what was expected of them and the doctor did what was expected of him. I was just supposed to fill in the gaps.

As the morning wore on, even the peached colored house didn't seem as pleasant and cool as I'd first believed. Working side by side with a man who seemed to go nonstop without breaking a sweat, I felt absolutely drained only two hours after stepping into his able little surgery.

Finally, he returned to the office, wiping his hands on another green towel. "That's the lot. Have some tea?"

I tossed the chart I was updating onto the desk and sat back in the ancient swivel chair with a groan, mopping my brow with my wrist. "That's it? Thank God."

"For the morning shift." He crossed the sill and, as an afterthought, reached back and held the door for me. "If we can arrange it during the warmest months, we see patients in the early morning and in the early evening. It's too hot during the midday for anything but emergencies."

"Oh, I see." I followed him down the narrow hallway to an enormous kitchen of blue and white tiles. It looked clean and deceptively cool. "And what do you do in the middle hours?"

In the process of pouring tea from a large glass jar into plastic tumblers, he shot me a look. "Sleep, if I can. Or study, or write chart notes." He returned the jar to the refrigerator. "If all else fails, I go to the mission."

I didn't realize that I had smiled. He was a religious man; my mother would be relieved to know that.

"Fr. Richard enjoys a game of cribbage every now and then." He set a tall, blue glass before me. "It isn't sweet. Will you take sugar?" I nodded and he pushed another plastic container toward me, before taking one of the blue ladder back chairs opposite me. "I would advise, Miss...Miss?"

"West," I supplied, suppressing a giggle. He had worked side by side with me all morning and didn't even know my name! "Heidi West."

He started to speak and stopped, both brows climbing up. "Like the little Swiss girl?"

"It was once my mother's favorite book," I explained, feeling as if there were something in his tone that demanded I defend my name.

"Very well, Miss West, I would suggest that you take your tea upstairs and try to get some rest." He waggled a finger at her. "Don't try to be efficient, even if, as I strongly suspect, it is your nature. Your unpacking can wait for this evening." He stood, his own glass in hand. "Come."

I picked up my glass and followed, once again a bit concerned about what lie ahead. In this case, it was a climb up those wide, tiled steps, around a corner, down a long open corridor with tall, narrow windows that looked out to the water, and a dark wooden door at the end.

Dr. von Hollow probably saw my reluctance, or perhaps it was his own that resounded when he spoke. "I thought you might be more comfortable here, away from…away from everything." He pushed the door open and stood back, allowing me to cross the threshold and enter alone.

It was a plain, white walled room, with a narrow bed, a small wooden dressing table, a highboy with faded, hand painted flowers in one corner and in the other was a small, drapeless alcove with commode, sink and the tiniest bathtub I had ever seen. The only color in the room was the cobalt blue of the coverlet at the foot of the bed and a milk glass vase of bird of paradise on the dressing table.

It was nothing like my lavender and eyelet lace bedroom at home, but it was adequate, with a wooden shelf mounted on the wall for my books and photos and a good sturdy chair near the window. It reminded me of the dorms at Santa Teresa, uncluttered, a good place to think. "Thank you." I inched further into the room and looked around and nodded in satisfaction. "Thank you," I repeated.

"Well, if you don't need anything else, I'll bring your bag up later," he announced. "Did you bring a bathing suit?"

Caught in the act of admiring the hospital folds of the crisp, white bed sheets, I looked back at him in surprise. He was younger than I had first suspected. I had it fixed in my mind that he was at the end of his forties, perhaps into his fifties, when we first met, but now, getting a good look at him in proper light, up close, he was barely halfway into his thirties. He certainly did not live up to my image of the Dutch; being tall, dark skinned, with a good, strong face, and deep set dark colored, wise eyes. Those wise eyes seemed to be searching me for things I didn't want seen by strangers. I wasn't as comfortable as I had been a moment ago.

He gestured toward the window with the glass of tea. "The mission has a small pool. In the afternoons, the palms shade it and it can be refreshing on days when it is too hot to sleep. Fr. Richard has given us an open invitation." He paused, giving me a chance to reply, which I did not. He shrugged. "Just something to think about." He seemed to sense my new appraisal and took a self-conscious sip of tea. "I'll call you at four. Surgery opens again at five but we'll have a light luncheon first. Get some sleep." He pulled the door shut.

Despite the oppressive heat, and the long flight, I was too wound up to sleep. Tea in hand, I went to the long narrow window, pushed the plain white curtains aside and looked out. My room did not face the ocean. Instead, I had a fine view of a cobbled courtyard, a small, well-tended garden of bright flowers, and the bell towel of the mission chapel, framed in palms. The pool must be beyond that, I decided.

Beyond the chapel, I could see a winding, black road that led to the only town on the island – according to Dr. von Hollow. I had learned enough from him that morning to know that most of the inhabitants of this little rock were farmers; tea, rice and tobacco were the principal crops. *You'd feel right at home here, Mother,* I thought, sipping my tea. I'm right in the middle of tobacco fields.

Thinking of Mother filled me with melancholy. Adele West was what was kindly called a faded beauty, a woman who lived in a past to which she did not belong. To her, life was still magnolias and southern belles. When her southern gentleman died without the courtesy of providing for her – or for me – Adele had been faced with the distasteful prospect of working for a living. She promptly decided I could do a better job of providing for our future. Researching the local environs, she set out to snare me a rich husband. The man in question was the most eligible middle aged bachelor in Savannah: Jarad Frampton, III, MD.

Through a series of coy and not so subtle maneuvers, Mother met the doctor and introduced herself, and then me, into his circle of friends, dropping hints about how well brought up and genteel I was, and what a fine wife I'd make for the right man. Her maneuvers were effective enough that Jarad and a number of his friends developed some interest in me. The only flaw in her plan was that Jarad made no secret that, if he ever married, he wanted a nurse for a wife. Thus, I was packed off to Santa Teresa Hospital for two years while my mother depended on the kindness of other strangers. It was an immeasurable blow to her plans when I took this position in Indonesia, instead. But…oh, what a relief for me.

"Of course, it's only for six months," I reminded myself, drawing up the rocking chair and rocking, sadly. A bright thought came to me. "In six months Jarad just might find himself another nurse – I mean, wife." I sipped tea, rocking, smiling to myself. "I can hope, can't I?"

Chapter Two
The Didactic

By nine o'clock that evening, I knew many things about the Dutch Doctor's practice on that tiny island in the Sunda Strait. The injuries and illnesses were generally not life threatening. Most of the residents rarely bothered coming to see him for minor things, and came only when something inconvenienced them; so the cases were mostly cuts and colds and the occasional concussion. The residents of the island favored bicycles for travel, but the roads did not, and many a pothole had sent a speeding cyclist headlong into a ditch. I learned that the patients had a strong affection and respect for the doctor, who was known through the many islands of the strait.

Most of all, I saw that children seemed to adore him because he bribed them with candy and praised them in that thickly accented, melodious yet stern voice when they were brave about inoculations and stitches. Although he could seem gruff and even impatient with some of the children, I couldn't help seeing that he watched each one leave with a look of affection, concern and pride. I learned that Dr. von Hollow's deep voice could be soft and comforting or as sharp as a scalpel. He was indefatigable, and he expected his assistant to be likewise.

I also learned that food had absolutely no appeal in such heat and humidity.

At the close of surgery, I put the last of the charts away, fanning myself with a folder. Six months of this, I reminded myself, dejectedly. And to think I could have stayed at Santa Teresa's, emptying bedpans, but in moderate weather and familiar customs.

"You didn't eat."

I jerked around in the swivel chair. Dr. von Hollow also had a surprisingly light step. "I...it ...was too hot to eat," I stammered. He had knocked at my door at four sharp but, by the time I had rinsed the perspiration from my body, dressed and found my way back to the kitchen, he had gone, leaving only a note that said there was a cold meat sandwich in the refrigerator. I opened the refrigerator and considered the fare, left on a dark blue platter, but I had the feeling that if I brought that invitingly cool meal out into the stifling kitchen, it would melt and become nothing but a soggy, unappetizing pool on the plate. I shut the door and went to surgery on an empty stomach. It seemed easier that way.

"You'd better overcome *that* quickly," he advised sharply. "What have you eaten in the last twenty four hours?   Did you even have breakfast today?"

I shook my head, too exhausted to calculate. It had been more than fourteen hours on a plane, two hours by water taxi, six hours in surgery, four restless hours in that stifling bedroom…no, the math escaped me, but I did know precisely when food had become the least of my concerns.

"Well?" he demanded.

I shrugged.   "Airline food," I answered vaguely.   That, too, had been completely unappetizing, but for entirely different reasons: It simply wasn't fit to eat.

"That won't do."   He pushed open the door to the hall. "Come. I'll boil an egg for you."

I laughed aloud, in spite of myself.

He turned and arched a brow at me.   "I said something funny, perhaps?"

"Well, yes," I admitted. "You know…a doctor advocating eggs."

He gave me a dark eyed consideration from shoes to cap and not taking any apparent pleasure in what I saw.   "You're young," he allowed. "Your heart can stand it. I'll make it soft boiled and slice up an avocado.   They are native here and surprisingly good," he added, standing back to allow me to precede him down the hallway. "You're American, I know, but your manner of speaking is strange to me."

I glanced over my shoulder. "Back home, we'd say you were the one who talked funny."

He didn't appear to take offense. "I am Dutch," he said with a faint but dismissive shrug. That was in his opinion, all the comment required.

"Yes I know." I took the chair he indicated at the long narrow kitchen table and sank into it with a grateful sigh. The table reminded me of the refectory tables where the nursing nuns of Santa Teresa ate, and just for a moment, I felt comfortable and at home. "They call you the Dutch Doctor."

"They?" he prompted, taking a small, copper bottomed pot from a hook on the wall.

"Your patients."

He nodded and nearly smiled. "And they call you Sister Lemon Drop." The almost smile disappeared. He filled the pot with water and delicately dropped in one brown egg. "I suppose because your hair is almost the color of the candy I give to the children."

I didn't smile with him. I was still a bit nervous about sharing quarters with him, but I didn't want to be accused of flying under false colors, either. "I'm not a nun," I blurted out. "It's true I came from a Catholic teaching hospital, but I'm not a nun."

As he looked over his shoulder with a jerk, the doctor's expression became a mixture of amusement and pain. "Are you trying to tell me something, Miss West?"

"No, I..." it occurred to me that he might have given my comments a different interpretation, and I looked away, acutely embarrassed. "It's just that you called me Sister as if I were a nun, and I..." I let it go, because I could see I was just making it worse. "Never mind."

He struck a match and lit the stove. "Miss West," he said with great equanimity, "here we call our nurses Sister. It is a common practice in Europe and Asia."

"Oh, of course." I should have known that. My voice became tart in self-defense. "Well, in Georgia, it is common practice to call our nuns Sister and our nurses Nurse."

"How very practical." He bowed slightly. "Very well, *Nurse* Lemon Drop." He opened the refrigerator and selected a brilliant green avocado from a dish on a shelf. "Georgia." He paused, considering the fruit in his hand. "That is in the southern part of the United States?"

"Yes. I'm from Savannah, Georgia." Glancing at my watch, I was, momentarily, rendered capable of doing simple maths, and accounting for time differences I managed to work out that I had been up thirty six hours. I felt that entitled me to a good, healthy yawn.

"Here, eat this." He set a plate of thinly sliced avocado before me. "It will keep you awake until the egg is done."

I obeyed, keeping my eyes fixed on the dark blue plate so as not to look at him. As tired as I was, I wasn't too tired to feel awkward sharing this domestic scene.

"So, you're not a nun," he said conversationally, winding the egg timer as the water began to boil, "but, you are Catholic?"

I shook my head. "Are you kidding? Me, from America's Bible Belt?" When I realized that meant nothing to him, I added, "Santa Teresa's the best teaching hospital in the state. I was lucky to get in, but it had nothing to do with religion."

He frowned into the pot. "That's too bad. Since you are living here with me, I'm sure Father Richard would like to hear confession from at least one of us." He took an egg cup down from the shelf. "I'll be frank, Miss West: you are not what I had hoped for."

As if he hadn't made that quite clear all day! I felt tears sting my eyes. "But, the agency assured me that my skills-"

"Yes, yes, yes," he soothed, quickly. "Your skills are more than adequate for my needs. But, *Nurse* West," he gestured with the egg cup, "This is hardly the hub of civilization. It's no place for a lively young woman. Did you not realize that when you signed on?"

Any tears I might have shed were burned away in rising anger. "Yes, I knew it would be pretty isolated, but I didn't sign up for dancing, shopping or shows. I came out to learn how to be a surgeon's assistant. And frankly, *Doctor*, I think your archaic attitude stinks." I stood up, trembling all over. "If you think, just because I've got hair the color of children's candy, that I can't be a good nurse, then just pack me up and send me back to the agency and do without for another six months." It would have been a perfect exit line, to pirouette with a toss of my lemon drop hair and disappear, but I didn't have the strength to do anything more than glare at him as the egg timer went off.

Dr. von Hollow's dark eyes had widened, alarmed at the start of my outburst, but now they narrowed, thoughtfully. "You made your point, Nurse," he said quietly and evenly, scooping the egg up from the boiling water with an expert dip of the spoon. "Now sit down and eat." He put the egg cup before me.

I remained standing.

He gave me an exasperated glower. "Eat or you'll be useless in the morning," he complained. He waited to see if I would respond to that. I did not. "Surgery starts at five," he reminded me with an edge to his voice. "You may have yellow hair such I have never seen, Sister, but I didn't bring you out here to look at it. I expect a damned good nurse tomorrow." And *he* turned on his heel and left.

I felt myself swaying slightly, and I gripped the back of my chair, staring at the place where he had been standing. "Impossible," I said, "completely impossible. I can't stay here, I'll go insane." But, hearing my own voice helped me push back the hysteria of exhaustion and frustration and the nurse in me told me to sit down, eat and get a good night's sleep. Everything would look better in the morning.

Dr. von Hollow did not need to wake me at four. The heat was already evident, and I had risen and bathed in the cramped tub, rinsed my hair and pinned it up, reluctantly putting on white stockings and a starched cotton uniform. Dr. von Hollow was surprised to see me downstairs within fifteen minutes of his knock.

He, too, had bathed, shaved, slicked his black hair back from his forehead and put on fresh cotton shorts and a white cotton shirt, which he would wear beneath his surgery greens. He looked me over from peaked cap to rubber soled shoes and then shot a glance at a plastic dish drainer where my egg cup and avocado plate had been rinsed and left to dry. "You're quick," he said, returning his attention to the pot he was stirring. "And neat."

Not having been invited to sit down, I remained in the archway, my hands clasped behind my rigid back. "Thank you, Doctor."

"Have some porridge?" he offered, indicating that I should take a bowl from the shelf. He must have seen the horror and revulsion rush across my face before I could school it away. "I know it's hot, but later you'll appreciate something on your stomach."

I moved obediently, suspecting that breakfast wasn't complimentary but obligatory. It was going to be difficult being o the job twenty four hours a day. I began to understand that living with him wasn't going to be arduous for fear of his making advances, but because he was just demanding. I would have to be on my guard at all times, not to earn his disapproval. Winning his approval seemed out of the question.

"After surgery, this morning, you must go over to the mission and meet Fr. Richard," he told me, spooning the thick, grey stuff into my bowl. "He's taken responsibility for you and he wants to be able to let the agency know you've arrived safe and sound. You'll like him even he is..." he paused, searching for a word, "a Yankee."

It took me a moment to realize what he had said; his accent made the word foreign to me. "Oh, a Yankee." I laughed, ruefully. "Oh dear, my mother won't like that."

He brought a bowl for himself and sat at the far end of the table as if to say he didn't eat with the help. But my remark must have intrigued him, and although he didn't look in my direction, he sent another question my way. "Your mother...what does she think about her daughter coming to a place like this? What does your father say?"

I spooned up steaming oatmeal and blew on it in a wasted attempt to cool it. "My father is dead," I said flatly.

"I'm sorry." He didn't sound as if he was a bit sorry that my father had died, only that he had brought up an uncomfortable topic.

"And my mother doesn't like this assignment one bit." The oatmeal scalded my mouth, but it burned away the bitter tasting subject of my father. "She wanted me to work there in Savannah."

The temperature didn't seem to bother him. He merely scooped it up and shoveled it in. "And why not?" he asked pragmatically. "Surely it would be more pleasant that Indonesia."

I put my spoon down, surrendering. There was no way I could eat that. "And what about you? Why do you practice here if you dislike it so much?"

I could see at once that I had invaded his privacy. He seemed to fold into himself, cloaking himself in disapproval. "I never said I disliked it," he said brittlely. He began to eat again, making it clear that all conversation was over.

I filed this information. I must never be personal with him. Not only was I supposed to be on duty twenty four hours a day, I was also isolated from any sort of company or companionship. I sighed in resignation. Five months and thirty days.

A few minutes later he stood pushing his bowl away, wiping his lips with a blue cotton napkin as if it signified that the meal was over. I stood, also, and carried my bowl to the sink.

"Leave it," he commanded. "I have a woman come in every morning. You weren't sent here to be anything more than a nurse."

I put the bowl and spoon in the sink. "Yes, Doctor." *Well, this has been a very enlightening morning, even if it was unpleasant,* I decided, following him down the hall. *I have been very thoroughly put in my place; I am to be a walking syringe and stethoscope and nothing more."*

"It shouldn't be too busy this morning," he told her a few minutes later, unlocking the office and turning on lights. "Today is Sunday. Most of the islanders are at Mass, and then spend the entire day eating and resting. Although most Indonesians who left behind tribal beliefs are Muslim, for some reason, the greater part of the people on this island have converted to Catholicism." He nodded toward a Crucifix hanging on the wall of the waiting room. "But they all, tribal, Muslim and Catholic, hold their traditions very dear, and Sunday is especially important to them – like a festival. They have parties or parades and theatricals." He smiled, and his voice softened affectionately. "You'll find a great love of celebration here. Between the Church and other faiths, holy days abound here, and if it isn't a holy day, it must be someone's birthday or wedding."

I wondered if his friendly and expansive manner as we prepared the surgery for business was his way of apologizing for his sharpness at the breakfast table, especially as it was clearly awkward for him to make casual conversation. "Their theatricals are something special," he continued. "It's how they share their history and pass it down to their children, particularly the *wayang*." He sent me a quick glance to see if I understood the meaning of the word. I shook my head.

"In the *wayang*, they use intricate shadow puppets instead of actors. Sometimes these theatricals go on all night. People talk and eat and nap through them because they know them all, but they love them." Almost as an afterthought, he added, "If you get the chance while you're here, you should attend one. They are quite beautiful."

I had seen pictures of the shadow shows with their elaborate and detailed puppetry in a magazine on the plane coming over, but I'd dismissed them as children's shows at the time because the article didn't go into much detail about their purpose and origin. Now I was curious but I wasn't sure when, in my twenty four hour duty day, I'd find time to see one.

As he took the time to show me around the surgery, the office and the supply room, he remained pleasantly impersonal, remarking only that, considering that I was thrown in with no explanations the day before, I did very well in finding things. He explained the bookkeeping procedure briefly and his filing system in more detail. He gave me a key to the offices and told me that on certain mornings I would be responsible for opening the office as he would be at the mainland, getting supplies and making rounds at the hospital.

I made notes in a little memo book. "What about house calls?" I asked, over the deep tolling of the Mission bells calling the penitent to Mass.

"House calls?" The idea sounded as foreign to him as the word Yankee had to me.

"You mean, you never visit a patient at his home?" I was surprised and a little irritated. How selfish of him! Surely there were times when a patient couldn't come to him. "What if there is a serious accident? What if the patient is too ill to come? What if a woman is giving birth?"

He did not show offense at my rebuke, nor was he tolerantly amused by my outburst. "Look around, Sister," he pointed to my little desk. "No telephones. If there were a serious accident someone would have to run here to get me and I would have to run back to them. It just saves time for them to bring the victim here in the first place, unless he absolutely can't be moved, which, in my experience hasn't happened.

"If a patient requires surgery," he continued, "we send him up to hospital on the mainland. If he becomes seriously ill, we put him in the infirmary at the Mission until he can be moved to the mainland, and either way, I would, of course, go there to treat him." He reached for a file, brushing past me, causing me to backpedal to get out of his way. "But to be on honest, on the rare occasion when there is no hope, the family tends to reject my treatment and call in priests or resort to the *jamu*." He shrugged.

I was feeling sort of foolish for having scrambling away from him when it was clear he hadn't even noticed me in his path. "Er...*jamu*?"

"That's *Bahasan* for herbal remedy...their own medicine," he explained patiently.

"What's *Bahasan*?" I asked both fascinated and irritated. I wanted to learn all I could about the culture and beliefs of the people with whom I'd be working the next six months, but not at the expense of getting an adequate explanation for his selfish behavior.

Dr. von Hollow drew a deep breath as if to commence on a length lecture. "*Bahasan* Indonesian is the official language of these islands. Every island has its own dialects, of course, but everyone also speaks *Bahasan*."

"Oh, I see. But what about-"

"And as for giving birth," he smiled as he realized he was cutting off my protest. "The women here take childbirth in their stride. Often they do not even stop their work until minutes before delivery. They really do not need me. Oh, now, don't be shocked," he scolded mildly, when he saw yet more protest in my eyes. "These women have a very closely knit network of family support. They would not waste my time calling me to attend childbirth. And, if the mother is Muslim, it would be unthinkable for me attend, anyway." He clicked his ballpoint pen and made a note in the chart in his hands. "If we suspect there could be a problem with the delivery, the mother is sent to Jakarta beforehand, where there are much better facilities available." He slid the file back into place. "So, no house calls."

I nodded, looking around the office. Something he had said at the very beginning of his lecture finally hit home. "No telephone?" I said. I couldn't imagine a doctor's surgery without a telephone. "Did you really say you don't have a telephone?"

"That's correct." He closed the cabinet. "As far as I'm aware, the only phone on the island is at the Mission. The communication network on these islands is very complex and effective without technology and- oh." He lowered his eyes to mine. "Do you have some beloved who intends to mark the passing months with long distance phone bills?"

"No." I tucked the key into my pocket. I think he was mocking me. "It just surprised me, that's all."

"Yes, of course. In the modern world, it would be unthinkable not to have a phone." Finally, amusement played in his eyes and around his lips. "This, Sister, is not the modern world." He pulled the calendar from the wall and studied it. For a moment, I thought he was going to prove to me that I had somehow gone back in time. Instead, he merely pointed to a date in the very near future. "I will be going to the mainland on Wednesday. I have rounds, and I will be following up on two patients, so I will need their files. I'll give you the information on Tuesday. I will also sending some mail and collecting some supplies. If you think of anything you need between now and then, let me know."

"Yes, I will." I pushed open the louvered doors that opened into the waiting room. An air conditioner would be nice, I thought, recalling the cool corridors and study rooms at Santa Teresa. Already the waiting room was an oven, even with the palm blinds down, but it was probably worse outside. I turned on the ceiling fans and stood under the spinning blades, wondering if the good doctor could get me a ticket back to Jarad Frampton, III, MD on Wednesday.

Chapter Three
The Daytime Drama

Like everything else I had encountered thus far in my trip, Fr. Richard was not what I had expected. From Dr. von Hollow's rather off hand remarks, I had anticipated a small, quiet, scholarly sort of man, in a long black habit similar to those I saw occasionally moving through the halls of Santa Teresa with expressions that mirrored their sorrowful purpose. Fr. Richard, however, was a big, brash ex-football player from New York, with orange-red hair, and freckles, wearing blue jeans, white cotton T shirt, and a long Crucifix around his neck.

I found him behind the chapel, raking palm fronds from the surface of the ancient cement swimming pool. He looked up as I pushed through the equally ancient white gate, and dropped the rake. "Well, well, well," he said in a booming voice. "You must be Sister Lemon Drop."

I liked him at once. He was not handsome, but there was something beautiful in his smile. "Fr. Richard?" I eased the gate shut to avoid another rusty iron squeal. "I'm Heidi West." I held out a hand. "I was told you wanted to see me."

"And how!" He came around the pool and extended his hand, his eyes full of approval. "Especially after hearing so much about you on the grapevine." He took my hand for just a moment, and released it, but I felt almost as if I'd received some kind of blessing in the exchange. "I just wanted to know you got in safely. Welcome to the Eighteenth Century, Sister."

"Thank you. It is a bit of a culture shock."

He laughed as I brushed damp curls from my forehead. "And I'll bet the weather has been a shock, too. Cheer up. We get fairly frigid for a couple of months each year. It gets down to a teeth-chattering sixty five. In this humidity, you almost expect snow." He gestured over his shoulder. "Come over here in the shade and sit down. We can at least pretend it's cooler here." He led the way to an iron table with several throne like chairs arranged around it. "We can talk." He waited for me to sit before he drew up another of the massive chairs as easily as if it were made of straw. He sat, hands on knees and grinned at her. "So, what do you think of Piers?"

"Piers?" Did he mean juries or wharves? I shook my head. "I don't-"

"I'm referring to Dr. von Hollow." His brow wrinkled up like a confused puppy.

"You mean, he didn't tell you his name? Well, that's just like him." He leaned forward to whisper in a conspiratorial tone, "He is a bit close to the vest, is our good doctor. Don't take it personally," he advised easily. "It's just his way."

"He…seems like a good doctor," I ventured. This big, robust, open man seemed to actually *like* the Dutch Doctor. Perhaps it was a mandate of his calling to love even his crankiest neighbors, or perhaps Fr. Richard was the kind of man not to see the evil in any nature.

Fr. Richard nodded enthusiastically as he straightened. "He is. The best. He left a thriving practice in Holland to come here." He gestured with a hand that seemed big enough to hold the entire island. "We're very lucky to have him."

A thriving practice? More information to file. "The patients seem to like him."

"They do." Fr. Richard was obviously proud of the doctor, almost as if he were personally responsible for having brought him to Indonesia. "The last physician we had in these parts was on the other side of the strait." He jerked his hand toward the water on the other side of the doctor's house. "He was so surly and uncompromising that no one wanted to make the trip to see him. He left last year due to poor health and we were able to get Piers. So, why weren't' you at Mass?"

I blinked sharply, wondering where I had missed the segue in the conversation. "I'm not Catholic."

He waved that away. "Well, you need to do *something*. You can't spend the rest of your life cut off from some sort of spiritual comfort and guidance just because-"

"Six months," I corrected. "I'm here for six months. It's only a training program."

"Oh." He appeared to be at a loss for words, and that appeared to be a rarity for him. Finally, he drew a deep breath. "Then, I suppose it would be silly to build a house for you."

"What's that?" I demanded, sitting up with a jolt. "A house just for me? Who would do that?" Did the doctor object to me that much? He'd only known me a day!

Fr. Richard nodded. "We would." The waving hand went back toward the white, stucco building behind them. "The brothers and I discussed it last night, when we learned you were…well, you weren't…"

"When you found out about the yellow hair," I concluded, dryly, brushing back a damp strand of the offending feature.

41

He nodded again, and let his eyes trip over me – very quickly. "And the great legs and the nice face-"

"Fr. Richard!" I was not flattered. "Why is it no one believes a blonde can be a good nurse?"

"No one doubts your nursing skills," he answered, as unmoved by my outburst as Dr. von Hollow had been that morning. "Piers told me last night that you were most capable. In fact, the problem isn't you at all."

I felt my brows arching up. "Is it him?"

"Oh, no, not really." He appeared fleetingly uncomfortable. "It's just the idea of a man and an unmarried, attractive young woman alone in a house all day and all night…"

I scowled at him. "Well?"

"Well," he shrugged, "things happen."

"Fr. Richard!"

"Well, they *do*," he insisted. "I may be a priest, but I'm not naïve. I listen to *The Guiding Light*."

"*The Guiding Light*?" I settled back in the chair with a thump. "The daytime drama?"

"Sure, everyone does. People say that we stop work in the middle of the day because of the heat, but the truth is," his eyes twinkled, "everyone goes home to listen to the soaps."

"But…how? Who has a television around here? How do you get any reception – especially for American television – you're in the middle of the Eighteenth Century," I argued. "You said so yourself."

"Oh, we don't watch. We listen." Fr. Richard pointed above the palms. There on the mountain that pinned that island in place, was a towering radio antenna, rising up like a giant, red and white magic wand. "A leftover from the war. Consequently, we get a lot of American radio, and a surprising amount of audio from television broadcasts."

I rubbed perspiration from my brow before it dripped into my eyes. "I don't believe it; no one has a telephone to communicate with their neighbor, but you can all listen to television and radio from a country half way around the world?"

Fr. Richard shrugged and chuckled. "I can't explain it, but that's how it is. Actually, we do have a telephone – only one on the island," he added, proudly. "We got it a couple of years ago. Of course, the connection might better with tin cans and a string, but at least we have one. Oh, do you like baseball? We get baseball from New York, and sometimes from Chicago, and last year we got one game from Los Angeles. I'll tell you, during the World Series, it's hard to get them together for Mass."

I continued to rub my brow, more in frustration than perspiration. "I don't believe this."

Fr. Richard leaned forward and patted my shoulder. "Feel like you fell through the looking glass?"

"Exceedingly more each moment."

"Don't feel bad, Alice," he admonished, "everyone does." He waved his hand once again. "This is Indonesia. It's a magical place. It will weave a spell for you, too."

I doubted it would weave a spell for me, unless it was a curse. "Well, this has been educational." I stood. "Was there anything else you needed? Any paperwork to be signed or anything like that? I should go back and try to get some sleep before the evening surgery."

"Oh, no." Fr. Richard stood up, too. I just wanted to be able to the Agency you got here all in one piece."

I gave him a little pirouette. "All pieces accounted for." I started to offer a hand, but something compelled to hold it up instead. "*The Guiding Light*? You're a priest, isn't that a bit...worldly for you?"

A little color crept into his face and he lowered his eyes. "We had been listening to a baseball game and the announcer said that it was coming up next. We thought it was a religious program."

I laughed. I couldn't help it. I didn't ask why he still listened to it.

He walked me to the squeaky gate, hesitating before he swung it open. "You're going to be all right over there, aren't you?" He looked a little anxious. "I would never call Piers anything but a gentleman, but he is a man."

I smiled confidently. "Yes, and I am a good girl – in any century." I slipped through the gate. "Good day, Fr., it was nice to meet you."

Half irritated, half amused, I walked back across the courtyard between the Mission and the doctor's house. *Piers* and the priest had evidently discussed me at some length, but what Fr. Richard had revealed to me helped me understand my boss a little. No wonder he was disappointed in me. He had apparently expected some sort of archetypal spinster; someone plain and sober with no illusion about her looks, the sort of female totally dedicated to her work. What an ignorant, sexist idea! I let myself back into the illusion of cool that was the doctor's house, taking care not to slam the door. Or maybe he thought a spinster, by his definition, would be no temptation. He was from Holland - had he never heard the story of the Ugly Duckling.

And who says, I continued in my mental tirade, *that a pretty girl has to be a wanton?* I was practically stomping as I reached the top of the stairs.

"Sister?" His deep voice came from somewhere close by. I looked around. The first door at the landing was open a crack, and the faint strains of a violin could be heard. "Is that you?"

I realized with a jolt that I was standing before his bedroom door, and I backed away. "Yes, Doctor," I answered, moving down the landing quickly, to get to *my* end of the hall.

The door opened all the way, and he appeared, peering around the doorframe. "Did you meet Fr. Richard?"

I turned around and, as I expected, he was frowning in disapproval at my shorts and sleeveless blouse. "Yes, Doctor," I answered crisply. "He seems very nice."

He nodded, his dark eyes straying back, almost longingly to his room, to the violin music. "Well, I'll see you at seven."

My hand on the hand painted ceramic doorknob, I turned back in surprise. "Seven?"

"Yes, didn't I tell you? We'll have no surgery this evening. It's a holiday so most people are at festivals and theatricals. But, I will have dinner ready at seven." He paused. "Unless you would like to make other plans?"

Now what other plans could I make? I wondered, annoyed. *I've been here less than two days. I've seen nothing but the Mission pool and the inside of surgery. Where would I make plans to go? And with whom? I've met a sexist doctor and a priest.* "No," I answered politely, "that's fine."

"Do you like Mozart?" he asked abruptly.

That would explain the violin music. "No." I smiled to soften the denial. "I'm afraid I like rock and roll."

He shuddered. "There's a Mozart concert on the radio tonight. I will be listening to that." He made a broad, generous gesture with one hand. "You're free to do what you like. Just don't stay up too late. There is surgery at five in the morning."

I nodded obediently. "No, I won't. I'll see you at seven." I went into my room.

My bed had been made, my uniform hung, my stockings put to soak in the sink, my cotton pinafore gown draped over the foot of the bed, fresh towels left on the shelf over the tub, and fresh bird of paradise left in the vase at my bed table. The housekeeper apparently did not observe the Sabbath. Now I had nothing to do.

I went to the highboy and pulled out my portable desk, intent on writing to my mother to send my cassette player and some tapes. I tried to make the letter long, describing the scenery without elaborating on the heat, describing the doctor without elaborating on his ideas, describing the Mission without elaborating on the priests' concerns and describing my room without elaborating on its location. To my dismay, I found I had only filled a page and a half. Well, it was better than nothing. I signed it, addressed an envelope, sealed it and put it on my bed side table, next to the bird of paradise. Perhaps the doctor would be good enough to mail it when he went to the mainland on Wednesday.

That done, I glanced at my watch and found I still had five hours until Dr. von Hollow called me to dinner. I was too wound up to sleep. It was too hot to go outside and walk on the beach, but it was a big house, there had to be some rooms that weren't too private for me to explore. I put the desk back in the highboy and left the room, taking care to be very quiet when I passed his room.

Downstairs, I began opening doors brazenly. Behind the door opposite the stairs, I found a little bathroom where I had changed into my uniform upon arrival. It was a long, narrow room, with all the functions crammed into one end, almost as an afterthought. It was next to the kitchen with its open space and long refectory table.

There was a small, dark, ornate dining room next to the kitchen, a room that, despite its unexpected elegance, was clearly seldom used. *Who would he entertain?* I wondered, with a shrug, and closed that door. Opposite the dining room, beneath the stairs was a small study with barely enough room for a desk and a chair. Just a glance told me it was very private and personal, so I closed that door and continued down the hall.

Opposite the doors to the surgery were double doors that opened into a large room with high, rounded ceilings, filled with floor to ceiling bookshelves, big comfortable chairs, several good lamps, well placed, and a fireplace. It was probably the only fireplace on the island that wasn't meant for cooking. In the corner, there was also a large, old fashioned record player, very similar to the one we had in the house where I grew up, courtesy of Mother's gentleman friend. It was a highly varnished oak, although the varnish had chipped away here and there over time, and there were water stains on the brocade speaker covers. There were large, old fashioned Bakelite knobs, and the lid was held up by brass, finger pinching hinges. Next to it were stacks of LPs and I went through them eagerly, but they were all classical performances. I turned my attention back to the books, only to discover that they were all either medical tomes, or written in Dutch and I suspect some were both.

One wall caught my attention, and I turned on a lamp to study it. There were dozens of pictures. Most were small, round paintings and sketches of Dutch scenery: traditional things such as windmills and tulips and ice skaters on frozen canals. I tried to imagine Dr. von Hollow skating along those canals and wondered how he could stand living in a place where the temperature never dropped below sixty five degrees. Each painting was framed in bright blue, and they were arranged haphazardly across the wall, as if to fill in places where photographs had been removed.

It was the photography that interested me. There was an older man with white hair and dark intense eyes. A young man was grinning behind the wheel of a sports convertible. There was a tall, peach colored house with a tile roof, which looked very much like all the other tall houses with tile roofs, all in a row along a canal. Among all these was a photo of the doctor himself, standing on a bridge, his arm tight around a lovely blond woman and two beautiful blonde children...

I stared at that photo for a long time. Fr. Richard had said the doctor left a thriving practice in Holland. He certainly left a country completely alien to this part of the world. He apparently left his home and other comforts. Why? Because of a woman? Because of a *blond* woman? Was that why he didn't trust my 'lemon drop' hair?

"Holland is a beautiful country, don't you think so?"

I jerked around, guiltily. Piers von Hollow was in the door way, dressed in khaki shorts, a white cotton shirt and a face full of disapproval. "I was bored," I admitted with a stammer. "I wanted to look around the house. I didn't mean to disturb you. If I'm intruding I'll go back upstairs," I lowered my eyes and added, "where I belong."

"You are not intruding," he said so crisply I knew it was a lie. "This is your house as long as you stay here. You can come in here, if you like. Only, there is not much entertainment to offer." He flicked a scalpel like hand toward the stack of records I'd so recently perused. "No rock and roll."

I felt the rebuke was not for invading the room, but for invading his memories. I decided to address the issue head on, and get it out of the way. "I was admiring the photos. They're lovely. Who are these people?"

He came to the wall, hands clasped behind his back, looking at the pictures as if he were the last man on the deck of a sinking ship, as he put his wife and children on a life boat. "These are of Amsterdam, where I grew up." He pointed to the white haired man. "My father. He was a doctor, as well. This is me." He pointed to the car. "When I came home from medical school." He shook his head. "I drove this car very fast."

I nodded in commiseration. "I drive too fast, too."

He looked down at me and then returned his attention to the photos. "It is because you are young. You will outgrow it. This," he pointed to the house, "was my house in Amsterdam. It was my father's house. It was my grandfather's house. All doctors. This door," he tapped the picture, "was the door to the surgery." He stepped away from the wall. "When I came here, I saw there was still much

Dutch influence here – especially on Java. I was inspired to build my house here as it was in Amsterdam." He shrugged. "I was laughed at, of course, but this house is much cooler than other houses here, even than the Mission, and certainly more stable that the hutches built on stilts you see everywhere."

I couldn't help noticing that he had ignored the photo with the woman and children. I knew that he knew I'd noticed. I hovered before the wall in uncertainty, not knowing whether I should press the issue or not. "Who lives in the house now?" I asked, taking the cowardly route. "Or did you sell it when you came here?"

"No, I kept it. It was the family home from the first stone that was laid there." He had gone to the stereo and began fiddling with knobs. "My sister stays there now." He paused. "She has two children; boys are far too lively for a flat. There is plenty of room for them there."

I looked at the photo again. No, I didn't believe that was his sister. If it were, he had very unorthodox feelings for her.

Noise burst into the silence. "Voila!" he pronounced, triumphantly. "Rock and roll." He strode out of the room without looking back.

Chapter Four
The Drill

Right from the start the days fell into a numbing pattern. Up at four to shower, dress and force down Dr. von Hollow's mandatory hot breakfast and tea, followed by a frantic four hours in surgery, dealing with everything from the life-threatening to the mundane in a steam bath. After a futile attempt to sleep during the worst heat of the day, getting up to a cold plate lunch, and enduring four or five more hours of surgery. The worst part came, however, when the last patient was gone, the office closed up and there was nothing left to do.

Immediately the door closed on the office for the day, Dr. von Hollow disappeared to listen to his classical music or play cribbage with Fr. Richard. He never lingered to discuss a case, or make suggestions or critique my work. He would simply pass me a nod as he walked out the door and that would be the last I'd see of him for the day.

Unfortunately, I didn't have the same opportunities. I didn't know anyone on the island except the doctor and the priest. I couldn't pick up a phone and chat with a friend from school, or watch television to take my mind off the heat, the rain, the mud and the long work day. I couldn't even sit on the verandah and listen to my mother talk about the way things used to be or, as she put it, the way things ought to be again.

To be fair, I wasn't completely without entertainment in the evenings. The doctor had thoughtfully brought back several novels and magazines when he'd gone to Jakarta. They weren't really to my taste being romance novels and fashion magazines, but I know he meant well. My mother, much to my surprise, had responded with uncharacteristic swiftness by sending music and my old textbooks, but still, the evenings could be long and quiet and lonely.

I had never been what you might call a social butterfly. I suppose I was as popular as the next girl, and had my share of parties and dates and dances, but they weren't the thing I lived for. After all, any romantic or social successes I might achieve would always be overshadowed by my mother's (real or imagined) conquests. If a boy showed some interest in me, my mother would either flirt with him herself, or chase him off. Now I searched my memories for something or someone to think about, and no one came to my rescue. The reality of it was that I'd reached this advanced age of twenty six and the only person I could really call a boyfriend was Jarad, and no one would call him romantic...he was more like a prospective employer. In fact, straining my memory, I couldn't recall a single time when he had made even the most remote attempt at flirtation. Marriage had been discussed in the very vaguest manner, but he had never even so much as kissed my hand!

So here I sat on my island paradise, too pretty to be trusted, but with no one to tell me I was pretty.

I tried not to dwell on the loneliness. Fortunately, I was never allowed to be moody or depressed growing up, so I never got into the habit. Instead, I used up my supply of stationery writing to everyone I could think up, used up all the thread in my sewing kit raising the hems of my dresses and shorts, and used up all my patience walking holes in the rug of my room. And I had only been on the island two weeks!

The next Sunday, I went to Mass, just for the change of pace and after services, Fr. Richard offered me the loan of the Mission's bicycle. Dr. von Hollow quickly put an end to my notion of getting out for some exercise, pointing out that I didn't know the roads and could easily get lost. So Fr. Richard invited me to come over during the mid-day rest and listen to radio with the brothers and the cleaning lady, but the last thing I wanted to do was become addicted to a program that had no basis in reality; where beautiful, wicked people fell in love or into bed at every station break.

Five months and eighteen days, I told myself, sitting on the garden wall late one evening, looking for some hint of cool air after a rain shower that had been anything but refreshing. How am I going to survive?

"Do you sew?"

I turned around with a jerk, nearly falling off the little brick wall that surround the rather ambitious flower beds in front of the house. "I can, a little." Hadn't he noticed that all my hemlines had gone up and all my necklines had come down? Well, no, *he* wouldn't.

The doctor was standing in the doorway, a shirt in one hand, a spool of thread in the other. "Could you manage a button? I'm hopeless with them, and I'm running out of shirts." He frowned. "I know it's a terribly personal request, but I'd be grateful." He held the shirt out to me. "If you wouldn't mind."

I swung off the wall almost eagerly, and picked my way across slick stones to avoid the mud. Even sewing buttons on the Dutch Doctor's shirts was better than doing nothing. "I hope I never need stitches while I'm here," I remarked tartly, taking the shirt and notions from him.

"My stitches are small and neat," he answered almost primly. "But, I've never once been called upon to put a button on one of my patients. Come in here," he stood back and held the wide, wooden door open for me, "the light's best in surgery."

I followed him into the office and was surprised to find that it was much cooler than the garden had been. I slid up on his examining stool, flicked on the high powered light he used and began unwinding the thread. "How did you do this?" I scolded. "It looks as if these were torn off in a fit."

"They were," he conceded, swinging himself up to the examining table. "A certain young lady patient objected to the idea of a tetanus jab, even though she had stepped on a rusty nail. She tried to prevent me from administering it by kicking, biting and snatching at my shirt front until my buttons all went flying. She still got her inoculation." There was a note of triumph in his voice.

You always get your way, don't you? I thought, filing that information. "Well, look at it like this: Your shirt was a hero." I licked the thread to coax it through the eye of the needle. I frowned. "This thread doesn't match, you know. It's going to stand out."

"Not as much as not having any buttons," he countered. "They won't come out even, either. I search the whole examination room after she left, but I could only find five of the six. Just leave off the one at the top. It will be all right."

I didn't mean to think about it but I realized that would leave his shirt open to the breastbone, and that would reveal...my mind somehow whirled into visions of brawny, brown chests such adorned the covers of my mother's romances. Drawing a deep breath, I tried to focus on my work. I don't think I'd ever thought such things before.

There was an awkward silence while I tried to find the place to match up the buttons, and he looked around for a subject to fill up that silence. "That package that arrived from your mother," he ventured. "All good things, I hope?"

I nodded, my eyes purposefully fixed on the button. "You mean you can't hear it? She sent my record player and some records."

"Oh, you got your rock and roll. No, I don't hear it, but you're so far away, and so quiet." He seemed to want to add something and thought better of it, leaving the words hanging, unfinished.

"I try not to disturb you." The first button was completed. "It's such a quiet house." I picked up another button. "I suppose that's what you're used to."

"No, not at all. At home it was always very noisy; people were always going in and out like a depot." He frowned again. "To tell the truth, I was afraid your mother was writing to encourage you to give up this assignment and go home. The way you've looked the past few days, I thought she had convinced you."

"The way I've looked?" I risked a glance in his direction. He had a peculiar look on his face; it was a combination of concern and complaint. "No, she hasn't said anything more than usual."

"Yet, you've looked rather unhappy," he observed with mild accusation, as if it were my fault I didn't enjoy living isolated in a steam bath.

I shrugged. "Not really. I just haven't gotten used to things yet. I will. Just give me a little-oh!"

"What is it?" he demanded, sliding off the table, and shifting to a professional aloofness. "What happened?"

"Nothing." I tried to hold my hand away from him as he reached for it. "I just pricked myself. I'm all right."

"No, you're not. Look, you're bleeding. Hold still." He caught my hand and examined it. "You gave yourself a good, deep jab. I didn't have so much luck with Mora the other day. Stop squirming." His fingers tightened around mine. "I'll put a little antiseptic on it and bind it up."

I let him take my hand reluctantly, and watched him work. He was completely in control when he had instruments and medicines in his hands, as if he could banish death, if he chose. He had a light, gentle touch that was very comforting. His hair smelled of citrus and soap and was very soft when it brushed against my chin. His lashes were long and thick and flicked across his cheeks as he concentrated on my wound. I felt myself growing warm…a different kind of warm, something not related to the steamy air around us. "I think it's all right now," I said shakily, pulling my hand back and easing away from the exam table. Unable to meet his eyes, I looked at the shirt, guiltily. "I'm afraid I'll have to finish this tomorrow."

He lifted his head and his dark eyes went over my face so carefully I could almost feel them on my skin. "You look pale. Are you all right?" He looked at the wadded cotton he had used to apply the antiseptic. "Did the blood upset you?"

"N-no, of course. I'm fine," I stammered, forcing a weak laugh. "What kind of nurse would I be if I went woozy at the sight of a little blood?"

"A very human one." Piers put a hand to my brow. "It's nothing to be embarrassed about. The heat plays tricks on all of us. Your skin has gone very cool. Come out to the kitchen and I'll fix you a glass of tea." He took my hand and without waiting for me to acquiesce, swung me up in his arms. "You're very light," he scolded, easing the surgery door open with his foot. "You haven't been eating enough. A girl with a metabolism like yours doesn't need to starve herself to keep a good figure."

He notices my metabolism, but I'll bet Fr. Richard had to point out my figure. "You can put me down," I insisted. "I only stabbed my finger with a sewing needle." I felt very uncomfortable and at the same time far too comfortable being borne through the house in his arms.

"Yes, only that, and then immediately when white, your pupils dilated and your breath got shallow," he countered. "A simple needle stick shouldn't make a healthy girl go into shock." He put me down in a ladder back chair at the kitchen table. "Sit still. You will drink some sweetened tea and go to bed. We will see about surgery in the morning."

"But it was only-"

He cut me off with a look. One of *those* looks; the kind mothers, nuns and schoolteachers use to their advantage. "You don't know that's the only reason. You may have contracted a virus." He opened the refrigerator. "You may be weakened from not eating properly. It doesn't look good for me to let my nurse come down with illness two weeks after she arrives." It should have been said as a joke but he wasn't smiling. He poured tea. "Fr. Richard would never let me hear the end of that."

"There's nothing for him to hear," I protested as he set a plastic tumbler before me. "I'm fine." Of course, I couldn't blame him for doubting me; I know I stammered like a fool and had gone a little faint, though it had nothing to do with needles or virus or food. I couldn't very well tell him that, though. What would he think of finding out his nurse was disconcerted by his nearness? Talk about never hearing the end of something! I took a big drink of tea. "There, I've had my tea. Now I'll go up to bed and see you in the morning."

He took a sip from the glass he had filled for himself. "Do you want help going upstairs?"

And be in his arms again? Oh, no. "I'm fine, I reiterated, standing. "I can get to bed on my own." Now I was blushing - I could feel it.

He could see it, too. He turned his back to me. "Very well. Goodnight, Sister."

"Good night, Doctor."

He didn't call me in the morning. The sky was going from purple to bluish orange in that spectacular display that was probably the highlight of the day when I rolled over and looked out the window. My first reaction was to close my eyes and be grateful for a few hours extra sleep. Lying there, however, I grew more and more irritated. What made him the authority of my life? Surely I could decide if I were capable of reporting for duty, especially in the case of such a minor injury. If he really thought I was so frail, he shouldn't allow me to continue in his service.

I sat up and dragged my fingers through my hair. The trouble, I acknowledged, wasn't the injury which made me appear frail, and no matter how careful I was, I wasn't going to be able to prevent that kind of frailty from manifesting itself again. It wasn't that I fancied myself in love with him – with *him*? What a notion! He was just the only man around at a time when my mind wasn't taken up with studies and other activities. It was like the imprinting that happens to baby ducks, and just as a baby duck will follow the first creature it sees, I knew I'd get a little faint every time I came in contact with the first man I'd ever really noticed.

Well, baby ducks eventually grow up and so must I. I threw the bedclothes back and got up. I bathed and dressed quickly, not taking the time to tie up my hair as I usually did, but came downstairs, pinning my cap into place as I hurried into the office.

He had gotten a little behind, trying to do everything himself, as I could see at once; files were piled up on the chairs and a stack of prescriptions were assembled in the middle of my desk waiting to be filled. I checked the names of the rather lengthy waiting list and began pulling charts when the doctor burst into the office. He skidded to a stop when he saw me, and sent his eyes up and down as if he had never seen me before. "Oh," he said, flatly, "should you be up?"

I held up my bandaged finger. "It was only a little needle prick, Doctor."

He looked at my hand, and then let his eyes slide down the length of my admittedly untidy curls. "Right," he said crisply, "who's next?"

I held out a chart and he stepped to the waiting room door. Hand on the door-pull, he turned around and looked at me again. "If you'll forgive a personal remark, your hair looks nice that way." He opened the door and called for his next patient.

I stood at the chart rack, my wounded hand pressed to my burning cheek, my heart doing a funny bump-bump in my chest, my knees just a bit weak. So much for that baby duck growing up any time soon.

Fr. Richard came at the end of morning surgery, and found me in the office, dawdling over paperwork so I wouldn't be forced to try and make small talk with the doctor over lunch. "So," the priest said, thrusting a collection of small white flowers in my face, "he let you up, after all."

I looked up and smiled, happy to see a friendly face. "It was a puncture with a sewing needle. A tiny little jab. He made too big a fuss." I took the flowers and sniffed. "So this is what I smell every night. They're lovely."

"It's star jasmine. And if it was just a tiny little jab," he demanded, "why did you go white and swoon?"

"I didn't!" I denied, annoyed. "He exaggerates. I've never swooned in my life."

Fr. Richard shrugged. "Maybe you didn't swoon, but he said you went white, and your breath got very shallow. Piers doesn't exaggerate. If anything, he's prone to understating circumstances, so when he said you got shocky and he was concerned, it concerned me. He's anxious about you, you know. He knows you're unhappy here. He doesn't want you to be making yourself sick over it. All you have to do is tell him."

"I'm not unhappy – or making myself sick." I shook a pencil at him. "And the next time you two have a heart to heart about me, you can tell him that."

"Very well, I will." He hitched his jeans and eased onto the counter beside me. "Now, let's play confessional. I'll be the priest and you be the penitent."

I sat back in my chair and considered him, amused. "Okay, what am I confessing?"

Fr. Richard gestured generously. "Oh, anything, anything that burdens your soul.

Why you agreed to come to such a far-flung place on such short notice, for instance?"

It only took me a moment to understand what he was implying. I felt color rushing back to my face, and my entire body growing hot with a completely different emotion. He thought I was pregnant and hiding out to keep from embarrassing my family! I would have laughed at the irony if I weren't so angry and humiliated. "Did he tell you that, too?" I demanded, slamming the pencil onto the desk.

"Oh, no," the priest shook his head, seemingly unconcerned by my rising ire. "I thought this one up myself." He gave me a half smile that I think he supposed was kind. "These things happen, Sister Lemon Drop."

"Not to me, they don't. I'm surprised at a man of God coming up with a notion like that!" I knew I was sneering but I could hide my disgust. "This is what comes of priests listening to soap operas."

"No, this comes of being a priest and taking confessions for fifteen years," he countered. "You certainly wouldn't be the first one to tell me something like that."

"And I'm not telling you that now." I sighed. "You did warn me that this was the eighteenth century." I rubbed my eyes, wearily. "Well, Father, you may tell anyone who is interested that I'm not hiding out until any sort of…" I lifted my voice to be heard out in the hall, "embarrassment has passed. I am a healthy, well-adjusted girl who came here because I want to learn how to be a good nurse, and this is where I was sent to learn." I pushed myself out of my chair. "I hope that doesn't disappoint you."

Fr. Richard shook his head, unconcerned by the possibility that he had offended me. "Oh, no, I can assure you I am not disappointed."

"Good afternoon, then." I took the jasmine and left the office. I realized that, from their point of view, it was a reasonable concern, but I was still angry and offended.

"Pretty flowers. You have an admirer?" the doctor observed from the kitchen, where he was slicing cucumbers for a salad.

I paused at the archway and gestured with the flowers. "Fr. Richard brought them to me just now."

He whirled around and stared at her. "Sister, he is a priest!"

Now I was really angry. I flung the flowers down. "Is that all you men ever think about?" I exploded.

He put the knife down and started toward me, his brow wrinkled up in bewilderment. "Sister, I-"

I wasn't listening anymore. "Honestly, I could forgive Fr. Richard for accusing me of being pregnant, he doesn't' know any better, but…you! You work with me. I'd like to think you've gotten some glimmer of my character and wouldn't think such things about me. Good afternoon, Doctor!"

Chapter Five
The Detour

The slamming of my bedroom door echoed strangely in the big, quiet house. So strangely that, when I got my breath under control again and wiped tears from my eyes, I went to my window and looked down. The echo I'd heard was the slamming of the front door as the doctor marched toward the Mission. "That's it," I advised bitterly, "go commiserate with Fr. Richard. He may be a man of the cloth, but he's got the mind of – of...a man!" I flung myself down on the bed and sobbed.

It was horrible, horrible! I wept into the pillow. *Someone actually thought that I...more than one person thought that. And that someone was a someone I wanted more than anything to respect me and my skills. How could I face him again?*

I pounded the pillow with my fist. *How could he think such things about me? How dare he?* I groaned into the pillow. My mother was right...all men think that way, and it's up to women to behave in such a way that they don't act on their thoughts. I don't know what was worse, that there were at least two men on this island who believed I had run away because I was expecting or that my mother was right about men.

I don't know how long I lay there, wrestling with that question, but the light had definitely changed through the window when I heard a light rapping on the door.

"Sister?" the doctor called softly. "Are you there? Miss West?"

I rolled over and stared at the ceiling. *Go away!* I thought furiously.

"Heidi?" He pushed the door open a bit and peered in. When he saw me, I glared at him and rolled over to give him my back. He pushed the door a little wider and came in. "I half expected to find you packing," he mused, shoving his fists into his pockets.

"You're not far wrong," I muttered toward the wall.

He hovered between the door and the bed, and I could actually hear the mental struggle he was experiencing. "Heidi, that was a terrible thing Fr. Richard suggested," he finally blurted out. "I'm sorry. I want you to know that I never entertained such thoughts. If he hadn't been a priest, I might have even called him out over it." He waited and moved a little closer to the bed. "As for what I said…I only meant it as a joke."

"It was in very poor taste," I told the wall.

"I agree, especially coming on the heels of his suggestion, but I had no idea when I said that." I could hear him pull my chair up to the bedside. "I'll tell you, Heidi, I have been worried about you."

I gave him my most baleful stare over my shoulder.

"Oh, no, nothing like that," he denied swiftly. "I was afraid you were pining for some fellow back home, someone that you thought you could tolerate being so far away from, and now you're lonely here. It's isolated and quiet. I'm used to it. I prefer it, but you..." he shrugged. "For you, it's different and it should be. You're young and pretty and –"

I rolled over and gave him a full scowl.

"And just because you're a damn fine nurse doesn't mean you're not entitled some sort of companionship, too," he finished.

I sat up, rubbing my eyes. "Doctor," I said coolly, "I think you've said enough. I'll see you this afternoon."

"No, you won't."

I watched him as he stood. "Why not?"

He rubbed the back of his neck. "You've worked two weeks straight without a day off. I want you to take the afternoon and go up into the town. It's no metropolis, but there's a nice park, and a sort of museum

73

of the local culture and a market to get staples: soap and paper and things. It's not exactly a holiday in Paris, but it's a change of scenery for you. Fr.Richard said he would bring the bike over as soon as it cools off a little. I'll draw you a map."

I considered it. I didn't like being sent out to play a pestering child, but I didn't like thinking of another afternoon cooped up with nothing to do, either. I didn't like the idea of going into a strange town by myself, but I certainly didn't want to go with either of the two men I knew. Finally, I drew a deep breath and nodded. "All right, I'd like that. You said there was a market, and I do need some things."

He frowned at me and then at the window, and I had a suspicion that he now regretted the offer. "If I didn't have surgery, I'd go with you and show you around, but'-"

"No, Doctor, that's quite all right," I said firmly, looking pointedly at the door.

He followed my gaze with his own. "Right." He looked back at me. "I'll see you this afternoon."

I wasn't exactly sure I agreed with the doctor's definition of 'cooled down'. It was still miserably hot as I wheeled the ancient bicycle down the last little dip in the road. The mile and a half ride hadn't helped me feel very fresh, either; my white cotton shorts and pink top were damp with perspiration and my hair was hanging limp and sticky around my face. Then there was that list of instructions from the doctor (watch out for potholes, I don't want to be treating you for something serious) and the priest (don't be too friendly, someone might misunderstand.) Still, it felt good to be out doing something besides waiting for the next round of work.

I had to concede that it was a pretty country, in spite of the miserable weather I'd encountered. The hills that surrounded me were deep purple and seemed so near I felt I could reach out and touch them. The fields were lush and green. Here and there a lone willow tree would twist and sway in a breeze that I never felt. Along the road other cyclists, accustomed to the heat and humidity, passed me. Some faces were familiar and those who had been to see the Dutch Doctor recently smiled and waved and called out something I had been told meant Sister Lemon Drop.

The town – well it was a village, really - was everything they had described it to be.

There were a few houses on stilts along a well packed dirt road, spread out before a common well. There was an open square draped in mosquito netting, surrounded by little shops that were barely more than boxes with bamboo curtains and tables of merchandise.

The place was bustling, though. People browsed the stalls, with baskets resting at their hips or on their heads. Children chased each other around the well, laughing. Men squatted under the mosquito netting, drinking from tea cups and watching the world they knew, and a few young men stood to one side, talking, glancing over their shoulders, gesturing fervently. *Young men, I realized, are the same everywhere. They all are ready to change the world, and when they aren't eating or pursuing women, that's all they talk about.*

I brought a list of things I wanted: thread, writing paper and envelopes, postage stamps (although neither the doctor nor the priest thought I could get them in town), some rubber sandals such as I'd seen many of our patients wear, a wide straw hat, chewing gum and a fan. It took a trip to every stall, and I never did find chewing gum – or anyone who knew what it was, for that matter – but I got everything else on the list, including air mail stamps. Each package had been wrapped almost lovingly in intricately woven bamboo leaf packages. I even bought a woven bamboo leaf bag to carry them in.

The sun was fading and the air was that blue grey color that comes between day and night, as I wheeled my bike back toward the road. The mosquito netted square was now lit with candles and people were sitting at small tables sipping tea or lounging on the grass, all facing toward one side, as if in anticipation. Curious, I stopped my bike nearby and watched, wondering what was taking place. Someone from within the tent recognized me, rose from a table and came to lift the veil of netting, beckoning me to come in. I hesitated for a moment, then put the bike's kickstand down and went inside.

The makeshift room was alive with chatter and laugher and people smiled at me as I entered. A place was made for me at a little table and I sat down, smiling back a little self-consciously. A glass filled with a brownish, frothy liquid was brought to me and several people turned to watch me, with anticipation as I sipped, tentatively.

It was a surprise. Smoky tasting, neither warm nor cool, it was thick and almost sweet, and not at all unpleasant after my long, hot afternoon. I smiled back and took a larger drink, and everyone around me nodded and smiled in approval.

It didn't take long for me to realize that I had come across a performance of the *wayung* – the puppet shows that the doctor had told me about. A large white cloth had been stretched across one side of the room, and lanterns were lined up behind it to give the sheet an eerie glow. One by one, surprisingly ornate shadows passed across the sheet, some encouraging shouts of pleasure , others boos and hisses. I didn't understand what was going on, but the images were pretty and my glass was repeatedly filled.

I was feeling awfully drowsy and the lanterns behind the sheet seemed awfully bright, when I finally tried to focus on my watch. I had been sitting there for more than two hours! Dr. von Hollow was not going to be pleased.

At first, I felt uncomfortable about getting up to leave, but a group of those young men I had seen earlier, had begun a shouting match in another corner of the room, and while attention was turned to them, I slipped out, clutching my purse to my chest. My limbs seemed to be made of rubber. As I reached the place where the netting parted, I looking around for someone to pay, but no one seemed to care that I was going.

Outside, on the dirt road, I blinked in surprise. It was completely black, with no light showing anywhere but inside the netting of the theater. I could barely find my bicycle and nearly dumped my packages trying to maneuver it around other bikes left carelessly lying about. Inside, the voices were getting a little louder, and started to take an angry tone. With a little shiver of concern, I climbed on the bike and turned in the direction I had come…I hoped.

I felt as if I had been riding for hours and almost completely uphill, when the poorly paved road came to an abrupt end. With a little exploration, I found I was at the bank of a stream, mangroves rising up like ladies trying to keep their skirts dry.

I turned around and looked down the way I had come, looking for the lights of the tea house, but all I could see were the silhouettes of mangrove trees in the moonlight.

"Well, this is just great." By holding my watch up almost to my nose, I was barely able to make out the time. It was nine o'clock! I had been gone over six hours. *The doctor is going to be furious with me*, I thought. *Well, it serves him right.*

With a sigh, I turned the bike around and slowly walked it back down the hill toward the town, looking for a fork in the road I might have taken in error.

"I can't believe how quiet this island is," I said aloud, just for the comfort of my own voice. "You would think I'd at least pass someone's house or hear a dog barking or something." The farther I walked, and the darker it became, and the quieter it was, the more I was grateful I didn't hear anyone else.

This time the road ended in a willow tree. I stared up at it, mystified, as if I had never seen a tree before. I certainly had never seen this tree. I didn't remember passing one so close to the road, or so big, or one that looked so spooky in the dark.

It was after ten, and finally starting to cool off. It was too cool, in fact, for my sleeveless terry top and cotton shorts. I shivered and rubbed my bare arms. *I want to go home*, I thought. *I wish I hadn't gone out to see the town today. I wish I hadn't come here at all. I wish I had never even heard of Indonesia. I wish I had never heard of nursing. I wish my mother had never heard of Jarad Frampton, III, MD.*

I turned the bike around again, walking much slower this time. *I want to go home*, I repeated, making a little litany to go with each step and the creaking wheels of the bicycle. *I want to go home.* I hit one of the infamous potholes in the road that made me lose my grip on the handlebars and the bike tipped over, spilling my things onto the road. On my hands and knees, I went over every inch of ground around the bike, finding, feeling to identify and counting up my purchases. The package that rolled the farthest was the one containing the rubber sandals. "What I should have gotten," I said ruefully as I piled everything back into the basket, "was a pair of ruby slippers."

Now the road ended at a rough wooden fence. At this point, I was convinced that someone was playing a great trick on me, moving the road around every time I walked it. "Well, I'm not playing anymore," I decided, putting down the kick stand and settling on the ground beside the bike. "I'm not going to move from this spot until someone puts the road back in proper order so I can go home." I rubbed my arms again. "But, I wish they would hurry up."

Sitting still, without the creaking of the wheels, it really *was* too quiet. And too dark. I began to hum. I looked up to count starts. I searched the horizon for something identifiable. Then I thought I had begun to believe in fairies. Off in the distance, small white lights bounced and played on the ground. *Fireflies*, I told myself. I rubbed my arms. *Or fairies*.

I hummed until I was hoarse. It was two in the morning. Occasionally, my fireflies would reappear on a different horizon, as if someone was moving them, too. The bike wasn't strong enough to support me so I couldn't lean back and rest. All I could do was think about the dark, and the cold and the lights and the fact that I was lost on an island in the middle of the South China Sea.

I must have dozed a little while, sitting up, because I woke sharply with the sensation of hearing someone call my name. "I must have been dreaming," I muttered, trying to see what time it was. When I lifted my head back to get more moonlight to fall on my watch, it seemed as if my fireflies were nearer and more defined. I watched them, trying to find a pattern in their movements, but they continued to bounce around at random. Too tired at that point to be frightened, I sat there, waiting for them to get closer.

When they did get closer, appearing to float up the road toward me, my fear did return and I stood up, nervously, my hands on the handlebars, prepared to make a ride for it if I had to. They got near enough to nearly blind me and I put a hand up to shield my eyes.

"Heidi?"

I lowered my hand in disbelief. I recognized that voice, even if I did not recognize the raw emotion in it. My fireflies were flashlights! "D-doctor von Hollow?"

"Oh, for the love of God, Heidi, where have you been?" The flashlight moved toward me quickly. Suddenly darkness scooped me up and held me close.

I could feel his heart thudding against my cheek and I could feel my tears burning through his shirt. "Oh, Piers," I sighed gratefully, "thank God you came."

He pushed me away, holding my shoulders. "I could just shake you. You scared me to death. What on earth made you stay out so late?" he insisted roughly. "And what are you doing all the way out here? Heidi, what *happened*?"

"Isn't it obvious, Piers?" Fr. Richard panted, running up beside us. "She got lost in the dark. And the way these roads twist and double back, it's amazing she didn't end up on Java." He stooped to pick up Piers' abandoned flashlight. "Now let the girl go before you shake what little life she has left right out of her."

The doctor eased his hands away slowly, as if expecting me to collapse when he did. I remained upright. My collapse had happened emotionally when I sank into his arms in joy and relief and sighed his name. "I'm all right," I insisted, turning my face to avoid the light. "Just show me the way back. I've walked up and down this road a dozen times tonight, and I keep ending up someplace else."

"How did you end up on this road to start?" the doctor demanded, hefting the bike up and wheeling it along between us. "You're on the other side of the village. Another mile or so and you'd have been half way up the mountain."

"I don't know," I confessed unhappily. "I guess I took a wrong turn somewhere. It was just so dark when I left the tea house. It caught me by surprise."

The two men exchanged bewildered looks. "Er...the tea house?" the doctor repeated.

I nodded. "You know, the one by the well. It was still so hot, and the place looked cool and inviting, and they were doing one of those puppet shows and...I just lost track of the time."

"You mean they had a theatre set up," Fr. Richard concluded. "Why would you call it a tea house?"

"Because they were serving tea there." I faltered on the roadway, looking back and forth. The two men had come from this direction, hadn't they?

"Tea?" The doctor dipped his head near mine and sniffed. *"Tuak,"* he said to Fr. Richard. "Sister," he continued crisply, "I do not want you to step foot in that tea house ever again."

I stiffened at his tone. Glad as I was that he had rescued me, I didn't recall giving him dominion over my life. "Oh?" I asked angrily. "May I ask why?"

The doctor looked at the priest. "We have our reasons," he said, pushing the bike along in determination.

"Fine," I snapped. "What are they?"

Fr. Richard touched my shoulder. "You didn't necessarily get tea in that tea house."

I skidded to a stop in the middle of the road. "What do you mean?" I gasped. "Are you saying I was drugged as I sat there watching a puppet show?"

Fr Richard patted my arm in what I suppose he thought was a soothing manner. "Not necessarily, Heidi, but it could have happened." When he saw that his words had done nothing to assuage my alarm, he added, quickly, "It's nothing to worry about. Honestly." He looked up at his companion, almost in appeal. The doctor kept trudging along. "You didn't do anything wrong. We just want you to be careful, that's all."

The doctor finally looked back at us. "You were very fortunate, Sister," he said in a voice that was not meant to be comforting. "Especially in that costume; it's very provocative and this is a very modest society."

I rubbed my bare arm, self-consciously. "You mean, they probably…got the wrong idea about me?" When the doctor did not look back to confirm my suspicions, I looked to Fr. Richard.

He just patted my shoulder again and reaffirmed, "You didn't do anything wrong."

I looked up at the black sky with its millions of twinkling bits of light. If I could have seen the moon at that moment, I might have howled at it in despair. I can't take any more of this, I thought miserably, I just can't.

Chapter Six
The Debriefing

For the second morning in a row, the sun was coming through my windows when I woke up. I struggled to sit up in bed and groped for my watch. It was after eight o'clock. Again the adrenaline rushed through me, but it was still an effort to move, and unlike the morning before, I couldn't seem to force myself to hurry down to surgery. Instead, I pulled my chenille bathrobe on over my nightgown and stumbled downstairs, in search of some coffee

There was none. On the table in the kitchen were two half full bright blue mugs, but they had been there when I dragged myself in just before four a.m. Apparently, Fr. Richard and Dr. von Hollow had been sitting up like fathers on a daughter's first date, and when I didn't make curfew, they abandoned the coffee and went out looking for me. There was no sign that Dr. von Hollow had been in the kitchen since.

Bewildered, curious and a bit amazed, I tiptoed down the hall and put an ear to the surgery door. It was silent. I pushed the door open. It was dark. I went through to the office; the waiting room was dark and empty, too. Taped to the outer door was a hastily scribbled note announcing that surgery was canceled and any emergencies should be referred to the Mission.

Well, this is a day for the books, I thought, wearily. Rubbing my eyes and stifling a yawn, I returned to the kitchen, lit the stove and filled a pot for coffee.

I heard what sounded like the back door creaking open but when I looked up, there was no one in the hallway. I went across to look into the waiting room, but there was still no one there.

"You shouldn't be up."

I turned around, irritated at his habit of sneaking up on me. The complaint died before it could reach my tongue. He was standing at the door to the surgery, uncombed, bearded and heavy eyed. His shorts and casual shirt were soiled and looked to me, in my bleary state, smeared with blood. He had never looked so tired, or so human. I felt peculiarly moved. "G-good morning. Would you like some coffee?"

"Yes, thank you." He pushed his hair back from his eyes impatiently and sent his gaze over my dishabille without taking any pleasure in what he saw. "Really, Sister you should have stayed in bed. After a night like last night, you need the rest."

"I know you think so." I filled my cup. "I saw that you canceled surgery. You shouldn't have done that for me."

"I didn't do it for you." He made an impatient sound. "I'm no kid anymore to be running around all night chasing girls, and then trying to work."

"Chasing girls?" I could believe he had done his share of chasing girls, and for some reason, it hurt.

"You know what I meant."

I brought another cup to the table. "I noticed you were up early enough." I looked at his shirt again as he settled into a chair and hunched over the cup. "Or did you ever go to bed?"

He didn't answer me, taking a tentative sip and running his hand over his eyes again.

"Well," I began, taking the chair at the other end of the table, "I'm sorry if-"

"It's not your fault," he cut me off brusquely. "I should never have sent you out alone. You didn't know your way around. You didn't know what to expect. You didn't know what could happen."

"You needn't make me sound like an infant," I complained.

He lifted his eyes from the cup. "If it's all the same to you, I'd just as soon think of you that way. In this country, in this culture, you are." He stood and strode to the refrigerator. "You didn't understand that certain practices are looked on differently…a woman on her own, for example…and they didn't realize that you didn't understand." He pulled the door open. "How are you feeling, by the way?"

"Very tired," I admitted. "Like lead."

He nodded. "That's to be expected. You'll feel that way for a day or two if you've never had *tuak* before."

The coffee cup slipped from my fingers and crashed to the floor. "*Tuak?*" I repeated in a gasp. "Is that like opium or something? I don't remember anything like that. I would never…I mean, I would *never*!"

He knelt and began collecting the shards of my cup. "Hardly," he said, disdaining either my ignorance or my carelessness – or both. "The narcotics use is surprisingly low in this region." He handed me a towel and gestured toward my lap. "*Tuak* is more like the native beer."

I hadn't noticed that I had spilled coffee on myself, and I began to dab at the hot liquid before it seeped through my thick robe to my skin. "I didn't drink any beer, either."

"No, you thought it was tea. It's fermented palm or bamboo – I forget which – but it is potent and its potency can sneak up on you." He stood, cradling the broken bits of the cup and carried them to the kitchen bin. "I made that mistake when I first got here, and I'll tell you I woke up feeling as if I had bamboo *and* palms growing out of my head. Fortunately, there are no dangerous side effects, aside from the usual foolishness which comes from inebriation. And you are never going there again." He looked at me, sharply. "Are you?"

I shook my head as vigorously as my condition would allow. "As Fr. Richard would say, 'And how!'" I looked at the towel in my hands and the brown stain spreading across my lap. "Oh, what a mess."

"Did you burn yourself?" He reached for the sash of my robe. "Are you all right?"

"I'm fine, I'm fine." I brushed his hands away. "Mine wasn't that hot, I had the cup half-filled with milk. It's just I was so surprised, so horrified by what you said."

He smiled. It was both a grim expression and one of triumph. "I didn't think you were the type to spend her time in bars." He went to the shelf and took down another cup. "What did you think of the town before they tried to get you drunk? Did you get your shopping done?"

I nodded, still dabbing at the coffee in my lap. "Even postage stamps. I just couldn't find any chewing gum. Now, I'm glad I didn't."

He chuckled. At least, I assume he did. His shoulders went up and down a few times. I had never seen him laugh. "I'll see if I can find some for you the next time I'm across the Strait." He brought me a half cup of coffee, and the pitcher of milk. "Well, this has been an eventful couple of days for you. Why don't you go on back to bed? A little rock and roll and bed rest might be just the thing for you."

I poured milk into my cup. "Well, before I decide, I'll see what restorative powers a cup of coffee might have."

"Oh, be indulgent just once. Take it up with you." He brought a broom from the corner.

"What about you? You're not going to stay up, are you? You were up just as late as I was."

"I'll be along." He swept briskly. "Don't worry about me, Sister, I know my limitations."

I stood, wishing he'd look my way so I could tell him how I felt. When he didn't, I sighed and picked up my cup. Something seemed required of the scene, so I said, "I'm very sorry you had to come and rescue me."

He didn't look up. "All part of the service."

The door flew open and Fr. Richard rushed inside. "You're back," he announced.

I frowned. Surely he knew that. My memory of the night's events were vague, but even I could place him there with the doctor on that long, uncomfortable walk home.

The doctor frowned, too. "Yes, of course."

"How bad is it? I picked up a radio report that said Sukarno himself ordered military troops to come-"

The doctor hissed sharply, and Fr. Richard looked at me. "Oh."

I felt alarm prickle my skin again...this was much, much worse than *tuak*, I could tell. "What is it?" I demanded. "What happened?"

"Nothing, Sister," the doctor soothed, then paused, thoughtfully. "It might be wise, Richard, if we could remove her to the Mission, or even off the island." He looked at me, with a false smile. "This really isn't what you signed on for, is it? No one would think less of you for leaving."

"Leaving?" I repeated, aghast. "Why would I leave? What is happening?"

Fr. Richard was frowning at the doctor. "It would be wiser for *you* to go, Piers. You know how Sukarno feels about Hollanders."

It was the doctor's turn to look aghast. "But, I'm not here in any political capacity, I'm here for humanitarian purposes," he protested.

Fr. Richard shook his head. "In this climate I don't think anyone's going to stop and ask why you're here."

I slapped my hand on the table. "Will someone please tell me what's going on?"

The two men exchanged looks: long, meaningful looks. Fr. Richard came fully into the kitchen and sat in the doctor's chair. "There's a little political unrest right now. The president of Indonesia has recently taken some actions that have a lot of people concerned. We weren't worried about it here in this remote place, but there's been a lot of violence and many arrests in the bigger towns."

"Last night," the doctor said, picking up the story, "some young men tried to start a protest in our town."

I thought back to the earnest, ready to change the world boys I'd seen in town. They seemed innocent enough. "Go on."

Neither man went on. Things were starting to be clearer, though. The doctor's weary appearance, the canceled surgery, the blood and dirt on his clothes. "How many were hurt?"

"A few dozen," the doctor answered, clearly upset. "Some children, too."

I pressed a hand to my mouth. "I don't understand why? It seemed like a peaceful Sunday afternoon when I was there."

"I don't know all that happened," Fr. Richard said, "but there was a disturbance during the *wayang* and some shouting and shoving began. And then..." again he paused and seemed to seek silent permission from the doctor.

Dr. von Hollow sighed. "Someone had a gun."

I nearly dropped my cup a second time. "Oh, no!" I settled back into my chair, shaking. "Nothing like that happened while I was there."

"Thank God for that," Fr. Richard said. "Of course, we didn't know that when we got the word. Someone was talking about it on his shortwave, and one of the brothers came over here to tell me. You weren't home, yet, so naturally, we were worried."

"Naturally," I repeated. I looked at the doctor. "And after you brought me home you went back to tend the injured."

He shrugged.

The implications of their words finally worked their way into my thoughts. "How many were hurt. Was anyone...killed?"

"No," the doctor answered, "but there were several injuries, some serious. I'll need to go back this afternoon to follow up."

Fr. Richard crossed himself. "Let me go," he offered. "If there are troops on the island you might be targeted."

"Why? Why are *we* in danger?" I asked, indicating the doctor. "We had nothing to do with this?"

"You don't know the political history of this place," Fr. Richard said patiently. "Indonesia was under Dutch rule for generations, but when Japan invaded during World War II, the Dutch withdrew. At the end of the war, when the Japanese surrendered to the United States, Soerkano claimed independence and resisted the return to Dutch rule. Shortly thereafter, he began establishing himself as a sort of supreme dictator, and there were a lot of changes made that were hardships for people here. Soerkano fears an attempted coup to reinstate Dutch rule, or even a new government without him."

I was stunned. Why didn't someone tell me I was coming into a country of political unrest? Everything seemed so serene here. Even in Jakarta, which had seemed so foreign to me when I arrived, didn't convey any sense of impending upheaval. I looked at the doctor, idly stirring his coffee, looking exhausted and concerned. "I can go with you, Father. I'm not Dutch, surely no one would look twice at me."

"With that hair? I don't think so."

"Oh, this hair!" I tugged at a loose tendril angrily. "I wish I was a redhead…or bald! Maybe then you'd take me seriously."

Fr. Richard looked surprised at my outburst. Dr. von Hollow sat up and flicked a thumb toward the door. "There will be no discussion about you going back into the village today. Or you, either," he said to Fr. Richard. "And it has nothing to do with your hair, Sister. No one's that superficial. It's just that you're tired and overwrought. A day of rest will do you good. Go on. Take your coffee upstairs, and get some rest."

I wanted to argue, but they closed ranks on me, and it was clear that any further discussion might be reduced to tears and hair-pulling. I think we were all tired and overwrought and they should have taken a nap, too, but of course, there was no telling them that.

I climbed the stairs, slowly. I was disturbed and it wasn't just the way I'd been dismissed, or the violence at the *wayang* performance, or even the new recipe for tea I had inadvertently tried. Perhaps it was that I didn't want to consider any of those things –

97

they were too big, too frightening, too *real* to deal with in my muddled state. So I floundered amongst other conflicting feelings, the way I clung to every word and gesture the doctor made, or the way I wanted to devote the rest of my life to looking at him standing in the kitchen doorway disheveled, weary and human. I felt so peculiar thinking about him that way and the way I felt when he laughed (or I thought he laughed.)   I ached when he dismissed me, calling me Sister as if my name had never passed his lips - as if he didn't even know my name.

Upstairs my packages had been left in a jumble on the dressing table.   I didn't remember bringing them home. I didn't even really remember coming to bed. I remembered trudging home in silence between them.   I remembered running inside the house in embarrassment and then hovering near the back door to hear if they said anything.   I remembered going into the little bathroom near the stairs and splashing cold water on my face and then...

And then I woke up.

I looked around the room.   My shorts and blouse were draped carelessly over the back of my chair, looking a little worse for the day's adventures.   My bra and panties were tucked under them as if hidden from view. I would never have left my clothes like that. Even my first night in Indonesia, when I went to bed too exhausted to sleep, I took the time to rinse my lingerie and put away my clothes. My mother would collapse in horror if I did otherwise – and trust me, even on the other side of the world, she would know. She might not comprehend politics or economics, or even understand why a woman would seek a career, but she would know if I went to bed without following the routine to which I had been raised.

Could it have been the *tuak* which inspired such sloppiness? Or had someone with less particular habits helped me to bed? I sagged against the door, mortified. The doctor had undressed me and put me to bed.

The mortification eventually turned to dismay. My body had evidently offered nothing enticing if he could continue to treat me so distantly and impersonally as he had just done. *He does think of me as an infant*, I realized.

I shrugged out of my robe and tugged off my gown to consider myself in the mirror over the bathtub. Somewhere in the night I had acquired a nasty little cut on my left shoulder and I had abrasions on both knees where I had stumbled, and a mean looking bruise on my hip. Still, if one overlooked the injuries, I looked nice enough. Granted, Marilyn Monroe need have no fear of me, I was definitely not sex symbol material; I did not have the full curves or the allure of bouncing flesh, but still there were *some* curves. I definitely looked female. A man ought to like what he saw.

Such contemplation embarrassed me, and I hurried to put on a clean nightgown and put the soiled one into the tub to soak. My thoughts were shocking - even alien to me. Because of my mother's obsessive drive to marry me off by playing up my feminine appeal, I'd always tended to downplay it, and now I found myself piqued because this taciturn Dutch doctor wasn't interested. *Good grief! When I got here I was worried he would make advances and now I'm upset because he's not.*

I tried to take his advice. I did listen to some rock and roll, and wrote a few letters and tried to remember where I'd taken a wrong turn on the road in the dark. I couldn't sleep, even though I tried that, too. Every time I let me eyes slip closed, the doctor's image drifted by; I could see the concern he showed when he found me sitting by the side of the road, the frustration in his eyes when I first arrived and he realized he wasn't getting a mousy spinster, the way he looked at me when I left my hair down one day.

He knocked on the door several hours later. "Sister? May I come in?" There was a pause, as if waiting for a reply I did not bother to give. "Are you hungry?"

I realized he wasn't going to give up. I put my book down and tugged the sheet up to my chin. "Come in."

He was balancing a tray in one hand and carrying his little black satchel in the other. "I thought I'd have a look at the cut on your shoulder," he announced, setting the tray in my lap before pulling up the rocker to sit beside me.

I inventoried the plate in a glance. Pears and bread and a very light broth, a cup of tea and a sprig of jasmine in a plastic tumbler. "Fr. Richard?"

He nodded, opening his bag. "He just called. He's concerned. It was his idea to send you off yesterday. He's doling out a very heavy penance for himself."

"Oh, tell him he's absolved," I advised, my hand, of its own volition, slipping up to cover cup my shoulder. "How did you know about the cut?"

I thought his face grew a bit darker. "I...um...noticed it last night...walking home," he said, after a moment. "I thought perhaps you'd fallen somewhere, but you were too upset for me to reopen the conversation for me to ask."

Well, that sounded plausible. "Yes, I was upset," I admitted, lowering my hand. I turned my face away and let him adjust the gown enough to look at the wound.

For a moment, he did nothing. It felt as if he were trying to look everywhere but at what was partially revealed by his maneuver. I suppose I was a little gratified that he had to at least acknowledge my womanliness, whether he liked it or not. I kept my eyes fixed on my lunch tray and remained silent.

He swallowed and reached into his bag. "It was a frightening experience, I'm sure." He had a cotton swab in his hand. "This might sting."

I drew a deep breath and let him dab the solution onto my shoulder. "It gets very dark on this island at night," I said, releasing my breath shakily. "It caught me by surprise. I don't notice it so much around here, going to bed so early with the lights of the Mission still on."

He nodded, his eyes on the cut. "I don't think you'll need stitches," he said, put things aside. "Yes, it does get dark. You can feel very lonely and insignificant here. Indonesia does that to you."

I shook my head. "I can't imagine you ever feeling lonely and insignificant. These people...they all love and respect you."

"Yes, these are good people," he conceded carefully. "I have come to have a great affection for them, too."

I turned my head and found myself meeting his dark eyes. They were so far away and sad. I knew what he was thinking about. "Why did you leave your wife behind?" I didn't mean to ask; the question was literally torn from me.

He pulled back, his eyes narrowing in indignation and pain. He looked at me a long time, full of accusation and recrimination, but I had made the blinder, I wasn't going to try scrambling away from it. I continued to look at him, waiting for his answer.

When he saw that I wasn't backing away from the question, he sighed and began to close up his bag with great deliberation. "It was the other way round, Heidi," he said slowly. "She left me."

Now I was ashamed. "I'm so sorry."

He screwed up his mouth as if to prevent more words – revealing words – from coming out. "It happens sometimes," he allowed, at last.

What a blow to a man's pride, I thought, morbidly intrigued. "So, you're divorced." I'd never known a divorced man. It was shocking, and a bit titillating.

His hands stilled and he looked up, his expression making his features look as sharp as knives. "I may not be Catholic, but I still believe marriage is sacred. I don't believe in divorce."

"Oh." *Well, so much for the childish fantasies I have indulged in,* I thought, both sad and ashamed. Unless…"And your wife? Does she believe in divorce?"

He snapped the case shut. "I don't think it matters here." His voice was as sharp as his expression. "Are you through examining me?"

I lowered my eyes. "I'm sorry. I shouldn't have pried."

"No, you shouldn't have." He lifted his head and skewered me with a gaze. "But since we're going to be so chummy and personal, perhaps you tell me who it is you are hiding from?"

"I'm not!" I protested, indignantly.

He shook his head. "Sister, if I'm to continue working with you, I have a right to expect complete honesty from you."

"And you've had it. I'm not…" I had to stop and reevaluate my position. "Not really." I sat up, pushing the tray away, rearranging the bedclothes, adjusting my gown. "There is someone…sort of…" I gestured weakly, "I can't explain."

"Try," he encouraged laconically.

I sighed deeply, finding more shame in the situation than I'd ever anticipated. "Jarad Frampton, III. He's a doctor, a general practitioner in Savannah."

"A doctor, of course." He stood, pushing his hands into his pockets. "Naturally, a doctor."

"Why 'naturally'?" I protested.

He ignored my question. "Continue."

"Oh, I know what you're thinking and it's not like that at all. My mother-"

"Yes, I've been wondering where your mother fits into all this," he murmured.

For a moment I thought I had said all I was going to say. I didn't like his tone, or the insinuations behind his expression. But still, words tumbled out. "She just wants me to marry well, that's all," I finished, lamely.

"For your benefit or hers?"

"I don't think that's very fair," I complained.

He made a face. "Very well, let's assume it's totally altruistic on her part. Doesn't marrying well include marrying for love?" When I stammered and stumbled in search of an answer, he barked, "Did she pick out this doctor for you?"

I didn't bother to answer that. I knew the pink in my cheeks had given all away. When I looked up and saw that bemused but triumphant look in his eyes, I felt compelled to add in as vehement tone possible, "But I like him. I really do." *No, I don't.*

"No, you don't," he countered. "Tell me, who will be happiest when you walk down the aisle with Jarad Frampton, III? Him? You? Or will it be your mother?"

I shrugged. "I'd like to think we all will be happy."

"Of course, you'd like to think that. You became a nurse just to please him, didn't you?" he persisted.

I bit down on my lip as I felt tears of disappointment well in my eyes. Did it really show that much? Was I so obviously not meant for this profession? Did I lack skill or compassion or-

"It was a good career choice, whatever the reason for choosing it," he said, softening

his voice with effort. "Unless you gave up something you truly wanted to do." There was a hint of a question in the corner of that statement.

I used the napkin from the lunch tray to dab at my eyes. "No. I like nursing. To tell the truth, I never gave careers much thought until Mother pushed – er, suggesting that I consider it. I've just been so afraid that I didn't have what it takes to be a really good nurse," I confessed in a rush.

"Never doubt that, Heidi. You not only have the basic clinical skills, but you also have compassion. That's vital. And," he smiled as he pulled the door open, "you know how to file properly."

I laughed weakly. So my education wasn't wasted. It was going to get me a husband. The only trouble was that it wouldn't the one I loved.

Chapter Seven
The Directive

A change came over the doctor's house. I no longer hurried in the morning to fill my stomach with hot cereal and my eyes with his presence. At lunch time, he always had something else to do so I ate lunch alone, as well. We didn't even exchange pleasantries in the office. There was no hostility, either. There was nothing.

The impasse lasted nearly two weeks. Even the patients seemed to notice something was wrong. Men raised curious brows at Dr. von Hollow, the women offered me sympathetic smiles. I was confused and embarrassed by the sympathy. I had no idea how the doctor dealt with the curiosity. Most likely, given his nature, he ignored it.

The most conspicuous phenomenon, however, was Fr. Richard's absence. The doctor neither went to the Mission for cribbage and counsel, no invited the priest to the house for conversation and coffee. The silence in the peach colored house was maddening.

Two Sundays after my tea house debacle, I sat out on the split log bench just outside the kitchen door, which was as far as I ever ventured toward the sea, watching the blues and greens of water colors spread endlessly before me. I was homesick, and yet to go home would break my heart. I just didn't understand anything anymore. Sometimes when I looked at the doctor's dark, impassive face, I hated him and everything he stood for: the heat, the isolation, the silence, the funny, achy, bump-bump in my heart. And other times, when I felt that funny, achy, bump-bump, I thought I could spend the rest of my life ding nothing but look at him...if he would only look back.

Sometimes it seemed he did look back. Sometimes, working in the office after hours, I could feel his eyes on me, and look up to catch his expression reflected in the palm-shuttered windows of the waiting room beyond my desk. It was a bemused expression, part wishful, part resentful and part confused. Whenever I saw that expression, for a moment I knew exactly how he felt, and then I didn't know at all.

As I tried to make sense of these nonsensical feelings that Sunday afternoon, I had that eerie sensation that I was being watched once again. I lifted my head and glanced around. The doctor was in the split door, leaning over the bottom half, his eyes fixed on me, unabashedly, but not necessarily with pleasure.

Fighting back that initial thrill, I twisted around to face him. "Did you need something?" I asked politely.

He gave me a thoughtful smile. "I was just wondering which would be better for you overall: to tell you there is a call coming across from Savannah, Georgia, or to let you miss the connection and possibly sever ties with Jarad Frampton, the third, for all time?"

Quite unaware that I had done so, at the mention of his name, I had straightened my posture and smoothed down my hair. "Jarad's calling here?"

He scowled at me. "Well, he's calling the Mission." He stood back and swung the bottom half of the door open for me. "Then I can assume you want this call."

"Of course!" I swept past him, trotting down the hallway to the front of the house. "Something might be wrong with Mother!"

"Of course," he murmured behind me. "I didn't think of that."

"Why else would he call?" I demanded, over my shoulder.

"Why indeed? When his fiancée is half a world away? When he hasn't spoken to her in three months? Why should he call now?" the doctor mocked, strolling along behind me.

"You're impossible," I snapped, jumping over a bed of crocus that did not stand much chance of surviving to the end of the year.

"Thank you." He stayed on the path and went through the little iron gate, but his long legs and easy stride kept him right at my sided as I pushed open the gate behind the Mission.

I was surprised to find his hand at the gate latch before mine. "What are you doing? Surely you're not coming along to listen in on my phone call?"

He shrugged. "I wouldn't miss such a momentous occasion for anything," he promised.

One of the Indonesian brothers met us at the back door, urging me along, chattering excitedly. To receive a phone call from a country 'half a world away' made me a celebrity, and everyone at the Mission crammed into the office to watch as I reached for the receiver, which was lying beside the ancient phone on Fr. Richard's desk.

"Hello?" I said, timidly.

My own voice echoed clearly almost a full minute later, disconcerting me.

"To speak to Miss Heidi West, please," asked a female voice in a very grave manner.

"This is Miss West."

"To hold on, please."

I held on, listening to the whining and whistling I heard on the line. "Hello, hello, hello!" demanded a voice that did not sound a half a world away.

"Jarad?" I gripped the edge of the battered cherry wood desk. "What's wrong?"

"What's wrong?" When Jarad was annoyed his voice became shrill, and it hurt my ears. It was shrill all the way across the Pacific. I pulled the receiver away from my ear. "It took me twenty minutes to get this call through. I thought you would have a phone right there in your room. I never had to wait twenty minutes to place a call in my life. For what this call is costing me, I should have reached you when I first dialed. It's outrageous."

"Yes, but I'm here, now. What's-"

"Where were you?" he continued. "Why did it take so long?"

I relaxed. My mother was fine. For all of his annoying traits, Jarad wouldn't babble on in a medical crisis. He would only babble on during emotional ones. "Jarad," I said patiently, "you must understand. There is only one telephone on the whole island."

"One phone? How barbaric! But, isn't the phone at the Mission? That's what I was told. Isn't that where you are at?"

"Umm..." I turned and looked at a line of faces and feelings, from awe to amusement. "Yes, but still, it takes a while," I lied. Well, I was at the Mission *now*. "What did you call to say?"

"I called because I wanted to get a progress report on your training. Your letters to your mother don't make mention of your studies and," he paused, putting his words together carefully, to convey meaning without implying promise, "I feel I have some investment in your educations." What he managed to convey was a threat.

I there hadn't been two priests, three lay brothers, a cleaning woman and an arrogant, know-it-all doctor standing there, I would have cried. But, because I did not have the luxury of privacy, I put on my best brave face. "How thoughtful of you, Jarad,"I said through clenched teeth. "I'm doing fine."

"And your training? Are you learning much about tropical diseases?" He sounded concerned, but not at the prospect of me being exposed to something life threatening. He was more concerned I was being exposed to something that was a waste of his time. "I don't think we'll be treating too many tropical diseases in Savannah. I hope you're studying more practical things."

"Oh, yes, I am," I said, my fingernails starting to dig into my palms. "Of course."

"Bookkeeping?" he suggested. "Are you studying the proper procedure for billing?"

Bookkeeping! What did he think I was going to be when I returned, a clerk? "Well, no. It's not really applicable, here. Besides, my work here is as a surgeon's assistant, not a front office nurse." From the corner of my eye, I could see the doctor's mouth twist up in a knowing smirk.

"I don't understand why you felt you had to go all the way over there to finish your training," Jarad complained, the shrillness returning to his voice. "There were a number of fine opportunities right here in Savannah. You could have stayed at home, and saved expenses."

"Well," I could feel my voice struggle to get past a massive lump in my throat. "That's a good point, but it's moot, now. How's Mom?"

"Adele is fine. She sends her regards. She wants to know if you received her most recent letter."

That was typical of my mother. How recent was recent? Did she mean the one I received two weeks ago, or was there another on the way? "Oh, yes," I said, anyway. "Thank you."

"What about medications, Heidi?" he demanded, returning to his original inquiry. "Are you learning to administer meds?"

"Yes," I said, acutely aware of the doctor's welling irritation. "Jarad, it was very nice of you to call, but-"

"And inoculations? They can be tricky for a novice."

"Yes, Jarad." *Oh, just once couldn't you say something affectionate? Say something that makes me feel like I am your fiancée, and not just an extra pair of hands? Jarad, please, give me a reason to look forward to coming home.*

"Some women just don't have the right touch for sticking patience," he said, in response to my silent plea.

The doctor lunched forward and grabbed my hand. "Sister," he barked, "you must come. There's a medical emergency."

"Jarad, I have to go. The doctor's calling me," I insisted, both grateful and humiliated.

"But, I still have –"

"Yes, yes, thank you for calling, and send my – oh!" The doctor gave my arm a jerk and the receiver clattered to the floor.

Fr. Richard bent to collect the phone, and stood, meeting the doctor's eyes with amused disapproval. "Medical emergency?" he drawled.

"Yes," he replied, unashamed, marching me toward the door. "He was in danger of rendering you absolutely useless. Good afternoon, everyone."

As he directed me around the pool, his fingers still tightly wrapped around my upper arm, I felt like a naughty child, caught at the scene of the crime, and being marched home to face punishment, and yet, I hadn't done anything more insidious than answer a telephone call. I didn't know whether to burst into tears or explode with fury.

I did neither until he had walked me all the way back to the house and pushed me through the front door. "Well," he demanded, releasing me at last. "Aren't you going to swell with righteous indignation and tell me I had no right to do that?"

"You had no right," I agreed, distracted. I had just peered into a long distance crystal ball and gotten a peek at my future, and it was dismal. I no longer cared how miserable the weather got, or how impassive and cool Piers von Hollow could get, I did not want to go home to that! I lifted my head and turned away. "No right at all." I walked away from him.

"Don't turn the icicles on me, Sister. I did you a favor," he called after me.

I didn't want to start an argument. I wanted to go up to my room and collapse in a pile of misery and self-pity, but I couldn't let that remark go unanswered. "A favor?" I turned back, slowly, a brow arched in surprise. "I don't understand that remark. You interrupted my long distance phone call, from someone very important to me, just to satisfy your whim. Tell me, how did that become a favor to me?"

"He's not that important to you, Sister," he argued.

"What right have you to determine who is and who is not important to me?" I snapped.

"All right" he crossed his arms over his chest as he leaned against the wall, "tell me that was the most romantic phone call you ever got in your life, and I'll get him back on the phone and apologize 'til the stars fall."

I matched his pose. "How do you know that it wasn't?"

"I was watching your face Sister. He nearly had you in tears." He unfolded his arms and took steps to be near enough to touch me. "Look at you now. You're still on the verge."

This is getting us nowhere, I decided, trying to reign in my feelings. "Jarad isn't exactly sentimental," I said, brushing him off as if he had actually reached out to brush tears from my face.

"I'll give you that," he agreed with a grim chuckle.

"You should know," I answered with a shrug.

He hissed like a wet cat. "What does that mean?"

I gestured airily. "He sounded just like you. Or…" I pretended to consider the matter, "you sound just like him."

"Nonsense, he sounded more as if he were quizzing you than wooing you."

That's exactly what he was doing. Why does this man have to be so exasperatingly right? "That was his way of…of showing his concern for me," I argued, wondering how he had put me into a position of defending Jarad Frampton, III. "Look, Dr. von Hollow, I know only acted in the best interests of your nurse, and I appreciate that, but I'm all right, and you were wrong to interrupt that call. You don't need to rescue me from people half a world away." He was smirking at me. "What?" I demanded, irritated.

"You said my name just now."

"Yes." I brushed hair back, irritably. "So? Am I not allowed to speak your name? Is it so hallowed?"

He continued to smirk. "You haven't said anything but 'Doctor' for days and days. I was starting to feel as if I didn't have a name." He shrugged. "But, just now you called me Dr. von Hollow. Very formal. You've only called me by my given name once, and it was on an occasion when I *did* rescue you."

The memory raced over my brain, making my thoughts sting; that dark, lonely night, when he appeared out of nowhere, like a firefly or a fairy, I threw myself into his arms, calling him Piers. "I..." What could I say? I could hardly deny that I had presumed such an intimacy, nor could I deny that he did, in fact, rescue me on that occasion. "I'm sorry. I had no right to...that is, you've never invited me to...anyway, I'm sorry."

His brows went up. It made his face look strange, as if surprise had no place there. "Why? It is my name."

"Yes, but where I come from, women aren't so familiar with their employers unless given permission."

He smiled a little and it didn't last. "Does that mean you call your fiancé Doctor, as well?"

I gave him an impatient look. "No, he told me I could call him Jared," I said sarcastically and reached for the stair rail.

"Has he ever told you that he loves you?" he asked, behind me.

No, I thought, pained, *no one has. And if I go home to Jared, no one ever will.* Forcing the hurt from my face, I looked over my shoulder at him. "Doctor, how can that possibly be any of your business?"

"The greatest healing power the human being has is to be of a healthy spirit and heart." He stepped up alongside me, dropping his arm across my shoulder. "If you are unhappy, you are also unhealthy. That's how it is my business. This has nothing to do with you being a good nurse for me. This concerns what your life will be like when you leave this behind." He gestured broadly with his free hand as if he could show me all of Indonesia with a flick of his fingers.

"For the record, outside of patient care, please call me Piers. And also for the record, Heidi West, you are entitled to be loved." He patted my shoulder and released me. Backing down the steps, he turned toward his study, leaving me gaping. "Good afternoon, Sister."

I remained where he left me, stunned, bereft, bewildered. The sensations, both physical and emotional, which washed over me when he so casually put an arm around me were so powerful that they blocked everything else, including his words, until he released me from is touch. And then, as that tide receded, his words and their underlying meaning rushed in to fill the void. *He doesn't think Jared Frampton, III, MD is good enough for me. But, I'm not good enough for Dr. Piers von Hollow. But, you're right about one thing, Doctor, I do deserve to be loved. It would be nice if the person I loved was the one to love me.*

One of the lay brothers came over the next morning with a message from Fr. Richard. Piers, as I now, quite deliberately, thought of him, glanced at the message and then at me. "There's a telegram coming over for you," he announced, with a hint of awe in his voice.

I was entering his notes into charts, but I put the pen down and made myself meet his eyes. "Should I go over to the Mission?"

He held out the message. "No, it's coming across by water taxi. I don't think there's been a telegram delivered here since I accepted this post."

"If they called to say the telegram was coming, why didn't they just deliver the message over the telephone?" I didn't reach for the paper in his hand.

"I don't know." The question annoyed him, as if he didn't like not knowing everything in the universe. "Maybe they didn't have anyone who could translate. Who knows?"

Naturally, the event was topic for discussion even among the patients, who chattered and peered out the windows from time to time, finally announcing, almost in one voice that the water taxi had arrived. Piers went out, himself, tipped the driver one dollar US, and brought the soggy brown and yellow envelope up from the dock, while I waited, hovering in the hall between surgery and the kitchen, wondering, of all things, where he got US money.

He walked up to me, as if he expected me to be there, and held out the unopened envelope. "It's for you," he declared, despite the fact we both knew that it was. Perhaps there was some local protocol I didn't know. I just stood there, holding it. He went to the surgery door, where patients had crowded around, watching, and shut it, gently. "Are you going to open it?"

I had never received a telegram in my life, and I would have been happy to go right on without every receiving one. My only knowledge of them was the belief that they only came when someone had died. I turned the envelope over and over in my hands, unwilling to open it.

"Steady on, Sister." The doctor took one of my hands in his. "Shall I call Fr. Richard?"

I shook my head, swallowing hard. Even his hand around mine couldn't prevent the fear of what was inside that cable. I pulled my hand free and tore the seal away, easily, drew a deep breath and pulled the message out. It read: NO PROFIT TO TRAINING IN ORIENT. SUGGEST YOU RETURN HOME AT ONCE. JF, MD

My fingers were trembling again. I felt hysterical laughter bubble up in my throat. Biting down on my lip, I looked up Piers. He wasn't reading the message, he was looking at me.

"Do you want to go?" he asked.

I shook my head.

"Good girl." He plucked the paper from my fingers and crumpled it into a ball. "After surgery, we'll wire back that I won't release you from your obligation, and this 'ardent lover' of yours will just have to wait the required six months for you to return home. Now," he tossed the telegram into the kitchen been and started for the office door. "Who's the next patient?"

I would have been grateful for the assistance if he hadn't deliberately found a way to mock and humiliate me just a tiny bit more. "I'll get the chart, Doctor."

Chapter Eight
The Dutchman

The days slipped back into a routine after Jared's call. It was generally and tacitly agreed that Jared and the celebrated phone call, and equally celebrated telegram, would never be discussed between us or with others. There was a subtle change evident in Piers' attitude toward me. He seemed to take interest in my efforts to improve as a nurse and caregiver. If I did something wrong he quickly, but gently, corrected me. He encouraged me to learn new procedures. He often left medical journals by my place at the breakfast table, and discussed cases with me over dinner. He even, albeit rarely, invited my opinion on some medical matters. His kindness, consideration and encouragement only served to convince me further that I had fallen in love.

His kindness, consideration and encouragement were limited to medicine, however. Whenever the conversation strayed to something more personal, he withdrew and became cool and detached, speaking to me as if I were a stranger. There were no more true confessions, no more expositions on the health of the human heart. And he never, *ever* called me Heidi.

Thus, every morning became a dilemma for me. I couldn't wait to get to the office, to be near him, to watch him, to listen to his voice, but I couldn't bear being close to him, knowing I had become nothing more than medical equipment on legs. I always went, though, and I always ached. Three months and twenty days to go.

The summer was nearly over, but the only perceivable sign was that it rained more often now. I could never get used to standing in bright sunshine one minute, and having rain pour down on me the next. The rain didn't serve to cool the air at all; it only added to the humidity. The ground didn't dry up as quickly between the rains, and now the walk to the Mission was a sticky mire of brown, tar like mud.

On the bright side, the flowers in Piers' garden responded to the increased moisture by bursting into an artist's palette of colors and fragrances all around the peach colored house. He liked to garden at night. I could often hear him humming Concerto Number Nine or Symphony Number Thirty Five as he toiled beneath my bedroom window. Sometimes I was tempted to peek out and watch him, but I decided it was better for my welfare to avoid the temptation.

Perhaps the flowers liked the music. I had never seen flowers in such shades of orange and blue and shimmering white. Every afternoon I would return to my room from grueling session in surgery to find the cleaning lady had brought a jar of ginger or jasmine or rain forced tulips of some brilliant hue to make my little bedroom a bit brighter, and at night I could hardly breathe for the sweetness of the air outside.

I had developed an understanding of baseball from Fr. Richard and mornings when the surgery wasn't too busy I would go over to the Mission to listen to the games being played the night before in the United States. Piers had Mozart, I had the Mets.

It wasn't just baseball we listened to, however. Sometimes we'd be interrupted with news broadcasts from China or Japan talking about the growing unrest in Indonesia. These reports were fairly alarming, especially since we heard none of this on our local radio. Sukarno was tightening the reins around the country, especially in Java and Sumatra and stirring up anti-Western sentiment, especially toward anyone who might have ties to Hollanders. When I tried to ask Fr. Richard if Piers was in danger, he'd cut me off with a firm comment such as 'He can take care of himself.'

Despite my Western background, however, ladies of the village and nearby farms had begun to seek me out for conversations. They taught me local lore and explained customs and beliefs, particularly the intricate interweaving of ancient, Christian and Muslim beliefs. None of them had anything to say about the political atmosphere there, and I knew better than to ask.

One of the women brought me a beautiful batik dyed sarong of deep purple and pale yellow and showed me its many uses, from dress to bedclothes, from veil to weapon (dampened and used like a whip); a sarong was an invaluable part of any Indonesian's wardrobe.

As the summer drew to a close I found, to my great surprise, that I had developed a life on the island and, with or without Piers, I was going to miss the place. Two months and nine days left of my assignment.

Fr. Richard had evidently given up his penchant for psychology, for he never again tried to probe into my feelings or the motives for my actions. Piers had apparently made it clear to him that all his original ideas and suggestions about me were unfounded and bordered on the ridiculous and if Fr. Richard noticed a change in me in the passing months, he elected not to suggest any possible reason.

I was grateful for that. If Fr. Richard had applied even the slightest pressure, my secret would burst out like air from an overfull balloon. Still, every time I went to the Mission to listen to the radio broadcast, I expected some little test, some coy question, some little, taunting probe. Instead, the test came from an entirely different direction.

Because the game had been rained out in New York, Fr. Richard was walking me back across the compound in the pre-dawn morning. He took a deep sniff of the fragrant air and sighed. "Monsoon season is coming, and it's early this year."

"M-monsoons?" I stammered. My knowledge of monsoons came from old newsreels in school and the eye witness accounts of a missionary at the hospital, seeking donations, all of which featured mass devastation. I had seen flattened towns and overturned ships. What chance did a little island village have against the full fury of Mother Nature?

"Oh, don't worry." The priest forced a laugh. "They hardly ever sweep this far down the Strait." The look on his face told me that he was very close to telling a lie. "They blow across the China Sea, into Java, not up this way."

I looked at him, doubtfully. "Even so, you must take precautions," I insisted as he swung the squeaky iron gate open for me. I thought of all those flimsy thatched huts, sitting up on stilts, near the village. They must be sitting ducks for a monsoon.

Fr. Richard shrugged. "We don't have to take too many. If the weather reports indicate that it's necessary, we board up seaward windows." He gestured carelessly toward the peach house. "Last year, Piers was still building, but he stuck to the first floor during the monsoons. That's the only tall building on this part of the island, the only one that could really be a target for a lot of damage." Realizing his gaffe, he hurried on. "We stock up on candles and batteries because the generators might go down. That's all."

I shuddered. "That's enough. What about the people in the villages? If the doctor's house is a natural target, how can their huts withstand the winds and rain of a monsoon?"

Fr. Richard rubbed the back of his neck. "The village is over in the valley. That's a natural windbreak for them. The only trouble they have is with the rain, but they're all on stilts, so they rarely get flooded." He felt he needed to add some kind of assurance. "And

I wouldn't worry about Piers' place. He had a Dutch architect come over to design the house. It's a good solid house and will stand for generations."

"Well," I passed through the gate and glanced out toward the water; it looked calm enough, "thanks for the warning."

Piers was at the door of surgery when I came inside. He glanced at his watch as he wiped his hands with a green cotton towel. "Is there something wrong? Your games usually last longer."

"Rain-out," I told him, my eyes straying left and right to consider all those tall windows that faced out to the sea. "What about you? I didn't see anyone in the waiting room. Is it a slow morning?"

He shook his head. "I've only had one or two patients this morning. It's probably the weather."

"Monsoons?" I asked, trying to sound casual.

Piers scowled. "I see that my good friend Richard has been talking too much again."

I looked up at the windows again. The sky didn't seem any lighter, in fact, it seemed darker now that the sun was rising. "He said they were coming early this year."

"It would appear so." Piers folded the towel over his arm and transferred his frown to it. "I was thinking, Sister…you have advanced far beyond the required residence training. Perhaps you should go back home now so you can take your exams and-"

I jerked around to look at him again. "Are you firing me?" I demanded, my heart thudding madly at the thought of leaving him. I was more afraid of that than the monsoons.

"No!" He must have heard the sharpness in his voice; for a moment his face registered surprise and then he softened his voice. "Not at all. If anything, I'm…" he searched for a word, "promoting you. You don't really need any further instruction-"

"I see." I nodded. "You're sending me home because of the weather."

He continued to frown at the towel. "I believe it would be the best thing, Heidi."

Heidi. My heart stopped thudding and melted into my shoes when he said my name. I pulled myself up, as straight and tall as I could be and said, "Listen, I'm from Georgia. I've lived through killer hurricanes, deadly heat waves, the people who are fighting for civil rights and the people who still think they're fighting the Civil War - not to mention my own mother offering me up as a wife to the highest bidder. I think I can ride out a little wind and rain here."

"A lot of wind and rain," he corrected, still avoiding my eyes.

"Maybe so." I crossed my arms over my chest and took a determined stance. "I'm not scared."

"I would never accuse you of being scared." He looked at me, at last, and there were so many conflicting emotions in his eyes I wondered if I had said too much. "It's not so much the monsoons I'm worried about." He paused, and I could see he was struggling to put words together. "This is a good solid house. We'll be safe enough. It's just that..." he paused again, and looked around. "Well, there won't be much to do. There won't be many patients, so I wouldn't need you in surgery. If we lose power, you won't even have your rock and roll."

"I'll manage," I insisted. Did he really have so little regard for me that he thought I'd hare out at the first sign of trouble? Or was there something that worried him? "Unless...will I be a problem?"

"No." He said it as if he didn't believe it. "I was merely concerned for your comfort and well-being. After all, as long as you are on this island, you are my responsibility."

And that's all I am to you – a responsibility, one who gets herself drunk and lost in the dark, the one who takes up careers to satisfy others, and one who falls helplessly in love with you and probably reveals it, somehow, every day. I felt tears of pure sorrow, but I blinked them away. I didn't want him to think I was afraid of weather or boredom or of him. "Then I'll stay. I don't want it on my record that I didn't complete my assignment." *I couldn't bear to leave you, please don't send me away.* I lowered my eyes because he might see the pitiful plea in them.

He was quiet for a moment, and then he sighed as if he had no choice, and no hope. "Very well." He refolded the towel and held it in both hands. "Could you put together some coffee? I'm about through in here."

"Yes...Piers." I waited a moment, wondering if he would respond to my use of his name, or study my face for a moment the way he sometimes did when explaining a technique to me, but his dark brown eyes remained fixed on the towel. I went down the hall feeling as defeated as he sounded.

He came in at the final perk from the pot, and I almost raced to fill a cup and put it before him. Catching myself behaving exactly like my mother, I reduced my gait to almost cartoon slow motion, wiping my brown with the back of my hand. "It's going to be hot today. Shouldn't it be cooling down a little? Even in Georgia it cools down when the weather changes."

"Not necessarily. I've never noticed it to be particularly cool at any part of the year. In fact, it was very much like this when I arrived here, last year." He used the hem of his cotton shirt to brush perspiration from his own face. "I think I'd been here three days when the first monsoon hit." He looked up, flicked a glance toward me and then focused on the refrigerator. "I suppose we'd better take an inventory of what we've got and what we'll need, and I'll go over to the mainland for supplies this afternoon. I have a couple of patients in hospital I'll want to follow up, and there's no sense waiting too long."

I got up and pulled open the door of the refrigerator.

"No, no. Nothing perishable," he corrected. "We'll have to make do with tins and boxed things for a while. If the generator goes – and it probably will at some point – we'll lose everything in the refrigerator. We'll need batteries, too." He got up and rummaged through a drawer to find a pencil and paper. "We should go through the house and check how many things need batteries and their sizes. What about your little record player. Can it work on batteries, too?"

I was opening cupboards, scanning shelves. "You make it sound as if we'll be under siege for months."

He shrugged. "Weeks, perhaps." He looked up at me. "Do you want to change your mind?"

I was tempted for a moment. Then I looked at those beautiful, earnest, faintly exotic eyes and decided that I wasn't ready to leave him. "No, I don't," I answered with renewed determination. "Sorry, Doctor, I'm just not a quitter."

For a moment, he looked as if he might smile. Instead, he picked up his coffee cup and sipped. "No," he agreed, "you're not."

It was after nine o'clock. There had been a few visits to the surgery, but they were all minor mishaps and things I could handle on my own. I would have been pleased with myself if I hadn't been so increasingly anxious about Piers. He'd left just before nine that morning and his round trips usually lasted no more than eight hours.

I tried to console myself with the knowledge that he had probably had to spend more time than usual at the hospital and getting the shopping done, but as I looked at my watch for the twentieth time since locking the waiting room door, I was facing something I couldn't handle, waiting for him to make the trip back. He was crossing in the dark with a rising wind that hissed through the palms behind the Mission. It was an eerie sound that shifted and changed with the wind; sometimes it sounded like fire crackling outside the tall windows of the peach house, and sometimes it reminded me of a local legend about the weeping of departed souls.

In the kitchen, I warmed the last of the coffee on the stove and drank it, trying to focus on its overcooked bitterness and not on my fears. I seldom went out on the beach, and never at night, for there were no lights and it was too easy to get twisted around, but that night I was tempted. I went so far as to open the back door and peer out toward the sea. After my experience in the village, I never wanted to get out of sight of familiar landmarks: those hissing palm trees, the peaked roof of the peach house, but when I did go out I was always struck by the complete emptiness just beyond that narrow strip of white sand. Usually, the waves that settled up on shore were so low there weren't even any white caps to show that it was water out there, and not the end of the earth. No lights shimmered across the water to reveal the islands that were within sight on the horizon during daylight hours. How in the world would Piers find his way home in that darkness?

Perhaps he didn't try, I decided, leaning against the door frame. There were whitecaps tonight, and they seemed unusually high. They rose up ominously and crashed down over the battered little dock. Piers must know better than to cross in weather like that. He must have decided to stay in Jakarta and come back tomorrow, in daylight. *Yes, that's what he did*, I decided, closing the door and returning to the kitchen.

My relief was short lived, however. As I finished my coffee and rinsed the cup, I heard a knock from down the hall. I was tempted to ignore it. Surgery was closed, but Piers would never forgive me if I let someone go in pain because of my adherence to rules about office hours. Besides, I realized as I came down the hall, the knocking was from the front door, not the surgery. I opened the door a crack and peered out. "Fr. Richard! What are you doing out at this hour?" I backed up to give him egress.

It had started to rain in just the few moments since I had looked out the back door, and the priest had clearly been caught in the deluge. "How's it going over here? I was listening to the radio and I thought I'd better get my supplies from Piers tonight," he answered, brushing rain from his eyes.

"But, he isn't coming back tonight," I told him, with a frown. "When did it start raining?" I looked past him, into the garden. "I hadn't heard it."

He shook his head vigorously and his thick red hair splattered rain water everywhere. "It just started as I came across."

I turned and hurried back to the supply cupboard next to surgery and got him a towel. "It looks pretty bad out there."

"This is nothing, believe me." He wiped his face and hands. "What do you mean, he's not coming back? I talked to him by telephone just after three and he said he was on his way to the dock then to come back."

"But, it's nearly ten o'clock!" I protested, showing him my watch. "Something must be wrong. It takes two hours in his motorboat."

Fr. Richard's broad brow was wrinkled up in concern. "Well, he probably changed his mind," he said finally. "I'm sure that's it."

Impulsively, I tugged at his hand. "What did you hear on the radio?"

He shrugged, innocently. "Nothing special. News, sports and weather. The usual."

"I would hate to be the reason for your penance tonight," I scolded.

"All right, all right," he surrendered heavily. "There was some sort of violence that broke out in Jakarta this afternoon. Military police were called in. Shop windows were broken, a bus was overturned. There were some injuries. I heard it on Japanese radio just now and thought I'd better get over and find out if he had made it home safe." He glared at me, as if to say 'Satisfied?'

"If people have been hurt, you know he would stay to help," I said, trying to sound calm and practical, as a nurse ought to do, but inside I was screaming, running in circles and pulling at my hair.

"Yes," he agreed, but there was something disturbing in his tone.

"What is it?" I demanded. "Do you think he was hurt? Do you...do you think he was targeted because he's Dutch?"

He spread his hands in a helpless gesture. "Sukarno is rousing a lot of public enmity against them."

"I never imagined these people, who all love him so much, could be prejudiced toward him just because he's white," I said, horrified.

He shook his head. "It's not racial prejudice," he corrected, quickly, "but political. The Hollanders held these islands for centuries. Sukarno doesn't want to give them any toe hold to take it back."

I stared glumly at the floor. I understood racial prejudice. I'd grown up in that awful stew. This, however, mystified me.

"It will be all right," he promised without conviction. "As you said, people love him."

"But, military police don't know that. And what about all the other-" A gust of wind hit the windows above us, making a thud and a crack that filled the hallway. "And if he is okay, and just running late, he's out there in that."

"It's nothing to worry about," Fr. Richard soothed. "You know he makes those crossings two or three times a month. He knows the waters well, and he's a champion sailor. He is," he insisted when I shook my head. "Go look at the photographs in his study. He sailed competitively when he was younger and won a lot of trophies." He reached out and patted my shoulder. "He was just delayed coming over. The stores must be full with panic buying. Don't get yourself upset." He patted again, awkwardly. "You know he likes you strong hearted. Do you want to come over to the Mission and wait there? He might phone again."

I shrugged his hand away, wretchedly. "No, that's all right." *Strong-hearted Heidi, that's me.* "When he comes back, he won't have to have to chase all over to find me. He'll be upset if I'm not here to help him bring all those things up from the dock. I'd better stay right where he expects to find me, Thanks anyway."

"All right," the priest sighed. "I'll come back in the morning to get our things."

"Good night, Father." I held the door for him and nearly had it torn from my hands. The wind was now blowing the rain almost horizontally. "Oh, my goodness," I whispered, putting my weight against the door. So the monsoon's arrived. Poor Piers.

Fr. Richard looked out into the rain reluctantly. He clearly didn't relish even the short trip over to the Mission in that driving rain. "Well," he sighed, "see you in the morning."

I nodded, vacantly, staring at the rain.

Chapter Nine
The Dictator

I wasn't sure what woke me. Opening my eyes, I lifted my head from the cradle of my arms on the table top. I listened, tipping my head to one side the way my old Irish Setter used to do. It didn't help. The only thing I heard was the wind pushing through the mangroves, like the wailing of departed souls, yet, something drew me to my feet, and I pushed away from the table and went to the window over the sink, peering out to study the darkness. I didn't see anything but ever rising white caps on black emptiness. I went to the back door, forced the bolt out and opened the door.

I only meant to open it an inch or so, but the wind snatched it out of my hands and slammed it into the wall behind me. After the wind came a sheet of stinging rain. I put my hands up to shield my face, and as I did so, I thought I saw movement somewhere out on that rain pounded sand.

"Piers?" I called out. "Doctor, is that you?" My voice was swallowed up by the wind. Impulsively, I got the flashlight down from a shelf near the door and grabbed my sarong from a hook on the bathroom door, heading out into the storm.

It was nearly impossible going, struggling down to the dock; for every step I managed to take forward, leaning hard into the wind, I would be pushed back two or three. I had wrapped the sarong around me to protect me from the rock hard rain, but the wind made a sail of it that nearly lifted me off my feet as it drove me back. The flashlight was useless, merely emphasizing the size and slant of the raindrops. The wind pushed the edges of the sarong and wisps of my hair around my face until they whipped my cheeks and eyes, and every time I opened my mouth to call out his name, wind and rain rushed in and stifled me.

Effectively blinded by the rage of Nature I stumbled forward, as the sand gave way under my feet, and the protruding wood of the wharf tripped me and sent me sprawling. The flashlight was jolted from my hands and went skittering across the planks to hit something several feet away. Belatedly, carried back by the wind, came soft, Dutch cursing.

It seemed to take superhuman strength to push myself upright as I heard, "Who is that? Who is there? Heidi? Is that you?" The flashlight was lifted and swung around to shine in my eyes. "Good God, Sister, what are you doing out here?"

"Looking for you," I shouted, trying to stand, and shield my eyes from the beam of light at the same time. "I thought I heard the boat. It's so late and the wind has been getting worse and worse. What happened?" The wind pushed me back to my knees and I elected to stay there for the sake of my grazed shins. "Where have you been? I've been – Father. Richard and I have been very worried about you."

"Jakarta," he shouted, straddling the dock and the boat and throwing boxes up onto the dock. "There was a bus accident." The wind suddenly shifted enough to pull the boat almost out from under his feet and he scrambled to hold onto the dock. "Get inside. You'll blow away."

I shook my head, even though I knew he couldn't see my denial. "I can't go in. You need me to stay. I'll help you get things inside."

He stepped out of the boat and straightened, tentatively. "I don't need your help," he argued as the wind shoved him forward.

"Yes, you do," I countered. "You can't carry all this stuff and the flashlight, too."

Piers swung the flashlight back in my direction. "Sister, you can't see two feet in front of you in this rain. You can't possibly carry things and find your way back. Go inside."

I shook my head again, attempting to brush wet hair from my face. "It's no use, Doctor, I can't even find the house without the flashlight. I might as well help you."

He was beside me, suddenly. "All right, all right," he sighed. "You can carry this." He thrust an oil paper package at me. "Tuck it under your wrap or something," he instructed. "Those are matches and batteries. It is essential that they stay dry."

There was something not quite right about his voice as he stood there, but I put it down to the extremity of our situation. "Yes, Doctor." I tucked them up under my blouse. He was providing a sort of windbreak for me, standing so near, and I had to gather all my wits not to touch him, to cling to him, to cry in his arms in relief. Instead, I adjusted the sarong in a knot around my shoulders and reached for the flashlight. "I was so worried about you," I whispered. I knew he didn't hear me.

He hoisted a box to his shoulder. "Lead on," he shouted in my ear.

I turned the beam of light back in the direction I thought I had come, and moved out bravely. Occasionally, beneath the thrashing palms, and wildly flapping branches of the mangroves, I thought I could see the lights of the Mission just to my left, so I knew at least I wasn't leading us right back into the sea.

It was a little easier with the wind at our backs even though occasionally the wind caught my sarong and let me sail forward a step or two, knocking me off balance. It still took us a long time to get to the back door, which now rocked to and fro, banging against the door frame and then the wall.

"You left the door open," he scolded as we reached the stone footpath at the back of the house.

"I didn't have any choice," I answered. My throat was beginning to hurt from trying to be heard above the storm, and his complaint, which seemed so trivial at the moment, stung. "The way the wind was blowing, I couldn't get the door shut as I left." I rushed inside and found a pool of water on the blue tile floor that spread into the kitchen and down the hall. "Oh, what a mess."

Piers was smiling grimly as he lowered the box to the floor. "A woman's mind...it never ceases to amaze me." He straightened and for the first time I could see him in the light. I gasped. His face was red and blue with contusions and cuts, one still seeping a tiny trail of blood from his cheek down his jawline. There was blood on his shirt, and his left arm hung so gingerly at his side it was easy to see he was favoring it.

"What happened?" I cried but didn't wait for an answer. I rushed toward the surgery door, fumbling with keys. "You didn't stay to help out with that bus accident...you were *on* that bus!"

"Never mind," he insisted, following me to the door, and easing the keys from my fingers. "Never mind that, now. Plenty of time for that once we get everything inside."

I held on to his hand. "What *happened*?"

"I told you. A bus accident." He turned away, shoving the keys into his pocket. "There are still more things to get from the dock."

"I'm coming with-"

"No." His voice was sharper than I'd ever heard before. "No," he softened it. "You're not. These things need to be sorted out. And..." he sighed, heavily, "is there any coffee?"

"No, but I'll make more, just as soon as I clean up this mess." I found the mop behind the kitchen door."

"Right." He reached for his jacket, always on the hook by the door, wincing as he did so. "We're sitting in the path of a major storm and you're worried about a puddle."

"Don't try to change the subject." I dragged the mop across the floor. "I want to know what happened on that bus. I'm no doctor, but even I can see that someone hit you in the face. I can see the details of someone's fist in that bruising. How major?"

Piers had touched his cheek, self-consciously but then brushed black hair back from his eyes. "Major," he said gravely. "While I was the hospital, I was listening to news reports from Japan. He said there are major weather patterns throughout the Pacific. Something to do with...have you ever heard of a term...*El Nino*?"

"It means The Boy," I said. "Oh! I think I know what you mean...there is a recurring weather pattern common in the Pacific, it happens once every six or seven years. It causes high tides and hurricanes and messes up migration patterns for birds and dolphins. I read about it in school. The South Americans, where it was originally noticed, called it *El Nino*, because it generally came around the same time as Christmas for them." I frowned. "But that would be summertime here, wouldn't it?"

About halfway through my dissertation Piers gave me a look that said 'Are you through?' "A simple yes or no would have sufficed, Professor," he said at the end. "There is an opposite phenomenon called *El Nina*, which comes around wintertime here."

The wind howled in the eaves as if to emphasize his words, and he looked up to the windows above them. "I should have boarded up those windows yesterday. Come pushed this door closed behind me."

"You're going back out there?" Beyond him, through the open door, I could see a mangrove bent as if bowing to the sea.

"There are things still on the dock, and I want to pull the boat up into storage. I can't afford to lose it." He flicked the flashlight back on. "Come shut the door now."

I moved. I hated to think of him going back out into that blinding, stinging wind and rain, but I hated more knowing that something had happened in Jakarta that was more dangerous than the monsoon. I also didn't want to contemplate the effects of losing that boat. "Be careful," I said, as if it would never occur to him otherwise. Even throwing my whole weight into it, getting the door closed behind him was a struggle.

I mopped up the pool of water and washed down the stucco walls that had been splattered with water and bits of debris. Then I began unpacking the supplies in the box he had left in the hallway. The contents of the box were disturbing, but I couldn't quite understand why. Piers did seem to be storing up for a siege. There were three boxes of matches (enough to light three thousand seven hundred and fifty fires, by my calculations), six dozen candles, four dozen assorted sizes of batteries, an extra, waterproofed flashlight, a roll of plastic sheeting, four five pound boxes of powdered milk, a box of penny nails, three five pound bags of jerkied beef and a bottle of brandy...and that was just in the boxes we had brought up so far.

I stared at that brandy for a long time. It occurred to me in all these months that, save the isopropyl alcohol in surgery, there hadn't been a drop of spirits in the house. This brandy seemed to be an omen. A bad omen. I put it high on the top shelf, out of reach and hopefully out of mind.

Piers seemed to have been gone a very long time. I sat at the table, poised to leap up and open the door and help him with his packages. Drumming my fingers on the table top, I listened to the wind, which had ceased its impatient whine through the palms and mangroves and was now howling and whistling around the eaves of the house. Just the sound of it chilled me and I began to shiver, teeth chattering slightly as I rubbed my rain soaked sleeves. It sounded fierce and frightening outside and the storm hadn't even reached us, yet. Or had it? How had

Piers come to have a fist in his face? What happened on that bus? The events at the tea house weeks before, and comments I'd overheard between Piers and Fr. Richard were starting to form an ugly picture, one far more dangerous than anything Mother Nature was planning.

Growing up in Georgia, I'd been aware of civil unrest. Of course, I never actually saw it, except the time when some drunken soldier tried to accost one of my fellow students, a tall, strong willed Negro who refused to back down. There had been no violence, but the air was full of emotion and had there been many more people around, it might well have deteriorated into riots. I knew what riots were; I'd read about them happening in Atlanta, and in other areas in Georgia, Alabama and Tennessee, but nothing like that had happened in Savannah at that point.

There had been protests when the woman had been accepted into the nursing program, and some families had removed their daughters, but the Sisters felt that Christ would have welcomed her and educated her so they would, too. That was the nearest I'd been to such violence, but that was near enough. What was happening in Jakarta sounded as if it could spill over onto our peaceful place, and that the

152

Dutch Doctor would be a target, much as Nursing Student Williams had been.

Piers had been gone over thirty minutes before I heard the shuffling sound dragging across the stone walkway. I jumped up, my heart in my throat. Listening to the sound, I could envision a mortally wounded doctor dragging himself back to die at his own doorstep, like a character in some macabre Saturday afternoon movie.

Just as my fingers reached the doorknob, the door flew open and slammed against the wall. There he stood, raining streaming down his face, one box tucked awkwardly under his arm, the rest of the supplies dragged behind him, arranged in a sling made from, I suspect, the sail he kept aboard the boat in case something went wrong with the motor. Wordlessly, he moved inside, and pushed the door shut with all his weight.

It wasn't until he had dragged all the boxes into the kitchen and began stacking them on the table that he looked at me. "Sister, you're soaking wet. Why didn't you change? You'll take a chill."

"I'm-I'm all right," I said between chattering teeth. "Let me help you."

"Don't be so selfish, damn it." He pushed me away from the table, and not at all gently. "Go upstairs and get into something dry."

"Selfish?" I echoed, backing away from him as if his words had made contact, too, and stung. "I was only trying to help-"

"Yes, and in the meanwhile, you will take a chill, and then I've not only got a monsoon to contend with, but a sick woman, as well. Well, I don't want that, thank you very much." He put the small box on the table with a bang. "Now, go. My God, don't you have any sense at all?"

He couldn't have hurt me more if he *had* struck me. With a sound that seemed a bit like a whimper, even to my own ears, I turned away quickly and ran for the stairs. Tears falling by the time I reached my door, I muttered mutinously, "I'll show him. He can put all that stuff away by himself. He can clean up that mess in the hall by himself. He can *contend* with the storm all by himself." Slamming cupboards and throwing clothes, I shed the sodden cotton shirt and shorts and filled the tub with hot water and a little of my precious bubble bath.

As the anger ebbed away, my common sense began to return. Piers was right. It was foolish for me to stand around in soaking wet clothing, especially in a state of stress and having been exposed to a sharp wind. I should have changed my clothes and dried my hair at once. Naturally, a doctor would be upset to find his nurse endangering her health. I would have chosen a nicer way to express such dismay, but he was a man of few words. He wouldn't waste them on tact when blunt force would do just was well.

As I relaxed, the lateness of the hour began to take its toll. I had been up nearly twenty hours. Drowsy and warm, I toyed with the scented bubbles, humming to myself, ignoring the wind that howled just outside my window, and the frightening threat of violence just off our shores, unaware of the voice calling my name, the step on the stairs, the faint, uncertain knock on my door.

"Heidi? Piers pushed the door open. "Heidi, I-" He froze in the doorway, speechless.

I stared back at him, just as surprised. My first reaction was to stand up and order him out of my room with an imperious gesture toward the door, but instead I slunk deeper into the bubbles, covering myself with my arms. "Would you please get out of here?" I asked in a breathless voice.

"I…" he had a steaming blue mug in his hand and he turned around, comically helpless, looking for a place to put it down. "I…" In surrender, he put the mug on the shelf near my bed and backed out, pulling my door shut with a snap.

I sat there a moment longer, not sure whether to laugh or cry, still seeing his face: part concern, part curiosity, part intrigue, but mostly horror. Finally, I climbed out of the tub, toweled off and slid into the flannel gown I'd left on my bed – the warmest thing I had with me. It wasn't very long, but it covered the essentials. I was brushing my hair when he knocked again. "Are you...decent?" he called, quietly.

I almost laughed at the shame in his voice. I reached for my robe and pulled it on, as well. It wasn't much longer, but the added layer would probably make us both more comfortable. "Come in," I called, fixing the sash tightly. *Why should he be so embarrassed? After all, he had seen me without the bubbles before. Or is it simply the fact that he knows this time I'm sober, and awake, and will know what he has seen?*

He opened the door, but did not come all the way inside, content to hunch against the doorframe, his fists shoved into his pockets. He looked terrible. He was clearly as exhausted as me, and his face was now several shades of purple. He still hadn't cleaned or dressed the wound on his cheek, but he had changed into fresh scrubs, so at least I couldn't see the gore on his clothing in better light.

He pulled one hand free to point. "I brought tea," he said in a flat voice. "It has brandy in it. That will help warm you." Tucking his hand back into his pocket, he let his eyes stray toward the bathtub. "And that was a good idea, too, taking a hot bath. Very smart."

I shrugged and put the hairbrush away. "That was my mother's idea. I mean, my mother always taught me to take a warm bath when I was in danger of a chill"

"Was she a nurse, as well?" I could tell he was trying hard to sound interested.

I rolled my eyes. Just the idea of Adele West actually *doing* something was quite ludicrous. "Oh, no," I said, remembering myself. "She just had a lot of old fashioned wisdom."

"Oh, I see." Just for a second, it looked as if Piers wanted to pursue the subject, but he must have decided it would be too personal, so he rejected it and continued to send his eyes around the room looking for reasons to avoid looking at me.

I looked at the sash of my robe. "Thank you for the tea."

He looked up at the shelf, where the cup still sat. "Here. Drink it while it's still hot."

I didn't move.

"Heidi, I'm sorry I spoke so harshly downstairs," he burst out as if the apology had been causing him pain. "I didn't mean to make you cry."

I opened my mouth to deny the tears but the expression on his face warned me not to try. "Oh, you didn't mean to. It's all right." I brushed at my cheeks as if I expected the tell-tale tears to still be resting there. "I'm not usually such a crybaby. Maybe the weather is making me a little bit moody."

"Or maybe someone took all his anger and frustration out on you when you didn't deserve it." He sighed all the way to the thick rubber soles of his canvas shoes. "It's been a difficult day. The water was very rough – even going over this morning, I knew we had some heavy weather ahead. And things are so tense over there. The tourists are in a panic trying to get out, and the media has whipped up a frenzy about the military actions against civilians, and then there was that incident…the bus accident." He rushed over the word, quickly. "All day long I was worried about your safety here, alone if the…storm should get here before I did. I just…" he tugged his hands loose and rubbed his eyes. "Well, it was unwarranted. Please forgive me."

I wanted so much to ask him what happened in that 'bus accident', but I didn't. I shrugged again. "You were right. I was being stupid and careless." I wanted to leave it at that but I couldn't bear the idea that he really thought I was stupid and careless, so I added, almost desperately, "It's just that I expected you to come right back in, and I thought you might need my help. I didn't want to waste event the time it would take to come up here and put on a dry shirt or comb my hair."

He nodded, grudgingly. "I know your motives were good. And thank you for all your help putting things away – but why did you hide the brandy?" he burst out. "I nearly tore the whole kitchen apart looking for it."

"I…" I didn't know how to explain my unease. "Of course I put it away." I lifted my chin a bit, defiantly. "At home, what little liquor we had in the house was always kept put away."

Piers frowned as if my words had accused him of something. "That might be true for social spirits, but not for this." He gestured toward the mug again. "This is…" he gave me a wry, half smile and my heart did a little fibrillation in my chest, "this is medicinal."

I made a face at him. "In all my life, I have never known an occasion where drinking alcohol had beneficial properties," I sniffed. "That old story about brand 'warming' your blood is nothing but an old wives tale. You ought to know that. All it gives is a false warmth."

Piers laughed outright. "Well, when this storm hits, and brings its false chill to these steamy climes, even you will be glad for some of brandy's false warmth." He looked at his watch. "It's terribly late, Sister. Go to bed." He smoothed irony from his voice. "Obviously there won't be any proper surgery tomorrow. We'll just be on call for emergencies, so sleep as late as you can. Good night."

I opened my mouth to ask about the bus accident, but he had already pulled the door shut. I had a feeling I had just witnessed his best effort at being tender and sincere but, and this surprised me, it was enough for me. I was still frightened, more by what had happened across the Strait than the weather, but I was too tired to give it any more energy until I had some facts. Ignoring the tea because I knew I could sleep without the help of the brandy, I shed my robe, turned off the lamp and slid under the bedclothes. Only three months and ten days left.

Chapter Ten
The Disaster

I didn't get to sleep late, after all. In fact, I didn't get to sleep through the night. Two hours after I turned off the light, a blast of wind bearing sand, palm fronds and mangrove limbs crashed through three of the four windows along the upstairs hallway. I woke with a scream, disoriented and scared.

A moment later, as I hunched under blankets, shivering, Piers burst into my room, letting the door slam back against the wall with another nerve shattering bang. "Heidi," he demanded, "are you all right?"

I lowered the blanket, jerkily, and found him in the middle of my room, in pajama pants and rubber thongs, waving a flashlight. "Wh-what was that?" I stammered.

"Windows," he answered tersely. "Along the hallway. Come on. Pick out some of your books and music and come downstairs. We're taking to the lower level until this thing blows through."

I slid from the bed and groped for my robe. When I picked up a stack of records, he added, "Put on shoes, Sister, there's glass everywhere."

I scooped up my own thongs, the ones I had purchased in the market square, and stepped into them. "All right, let's go."

Outside my door, it was a disaster. Seaweed, palm fronds, sand, water and glass were strewn everywhere, up and down the landing, and splattered against the wide, white walls. Wind raged through the gaping holes where the windows used to be. Fragments of glass still clung to the casings, threatening to fly off and embed themselves in the walls like darts. Piers urged me down the corridor to the stairs, shielding me with his body.

We took refuge in the living room, which was facing away from the water. Piers had risked a foray into the kitchen, so there was a Thermos of the coffee I'd made the night before, two bottles filled with water, jerkied beef and a few cans of fruit. He had started a fire in that eccentric wood stove of his, and pulled one of the settees up close to it for me.

I remembered the first day I had come to the big peach house, laughing at the notion that a man would have a fireplace in this environment, but at that moment, with the wind roaring overhead, I sat down, grateful for the warmth. "Should we be at ground level? Is it safe?" I didn't really want to go back upstairs past those gaping, empty windows, but at the same time, I couldn't help thinking that we were the only place on the island not on stilts.

Piers nodded, arranging supplies on the table the way he would set up instruments for a surgery. "The foundation of this house has an excellent drainage system so there's little danger of flooding. More importantly, this room has no sea facing window, so we're not likely to have smashed glass falling down on us. This way, if someone does come here for help, somehow," he shrugged at the fantastic possibility, "then we won't be trapped up there and unable to get to them. Don't worry…we're safe from the storm here."

Upstairs, the wind renewed its howling, whining through the shattered windows. I shuddered at the sound. "Does this happen every year?" I asked, pushing my hands toward the stove. They were shaking. I was still jarred by the explosion that woke me.

"I don't know." Piers shook his head as he poked a stick of kindling into the fire. "The house wasn't completed last year. Those windows upstairs were still boarded up because the glass hadn't been delivered. There was some minor damage to the roof and around the eaves, but the windows didn't blast out like that." He shook his head again.

"It's my fault. I should have gotten them boarded up a week ago."

"Father Richard said the storms came early this year," I countered. "How could you know that would happen?"

Piers considered the kindling in his hands. "There was a feeling in the air, even last week. Several of our patients mentioned it, but I had my mind on other things." He sat back on the floor, a crocheted afghan draped over his bare shoulders. "I'm usually much better prepared for crises."

I could see that he was trying to reassure me – or perhaps he was trying to reassure himself. "It's part of medical training, I suppose. While I was at Santa Theresa, I was sent to the Emergency Room of City Hospital for experience. After a week there, I found I was almost sleeping with one eye open, waiting for disaster. There was a pretty big hurricane while I was on duty there," I added, trying to sound confident and reassuring when I was actually a bit frightened by the memories of Hurricane Gracie and the damage wrought all around us.

Piers looked over his shoulder at the shuttered windows of the front room, listening to the lashing wind and debris against them. "In Amsterdam, the concern is always for rising water, not wind." He lifted a hand and pointed at the photos on the wall behind me. "That house, it's on a canal, like so many houses there. We've been flooded six times in that house that I can remember, and who knows how many times before me. Killer floods." He reached for his coffee cup. "I suppose it is all a matter of what you're used to."

I pulled my robe tighter around me. "Well, I don't know if I'll ever be used to monsoons – the hot and cold together like that…it's a little exotic for me."

Piers sighed heavily into his coffee cup. "I know," he said, "I should have sent you home weeks ago."

I stiffened at his tone. "Oh, I see, you think I'm a coward. Well, let me tell you, Doctor Everything's-Under-Control: I'm as tough as they come. My family has faced droughts, floods, poverty, the Yankee Army *and* hurricanes. This isn't going to scare me into running home to Momma. *You* aren't going to scare me into running home to Momma. I came here for six months and I'm *staying*." I slapped my hands against the table between us for emphasis.

Piers had started an argument about halfway into my speech, but fell silent to let me rant on. Finally, he looked up. "Are you through? Good. Then let me tell you something, Miss Tough-As-They-Come: I never said I thought you were a coward. Cowards wouldn't leave home to spend six months in an alien part of the world. Cowards wouldn't even consider living in a strange man's house, on an island where she was the only non-native woman. Cowards, Nurse West, wouldn't go into nursing at all, no matter what their motivation might be." With that, he unfolded his legs and stood, letting the afghan fall to the floor. "I'm going to check the doors in back."

I sat stunned, emotionally staggered by his outburst. I didn't know what to think of his speech. Did he have regard for me...or contempt? Did he admire my avocation without admiring me personally? Did he, in spite of all he had just said, still wish he had sent me back weeks ago? Did I wish I had gone? I drank coffee, not caring that it had grown cold and bitter. My mind remained riveted on his expression during that speech; his dark eyes had blazed and his face flushed. There was so much feeling in him, but what *kind* of feeling?

"The back sill has overrun and there's another mess in the hall," he announced from the doorway. "Can you round up towels from the laundry so we can stop up that sill?" He waited a beat. "Sister?"

I jerked into motion. For a moment, all I could do was take in the sight of him, bare-chested, in the doorway. He had a magnificent physique, I realized with an absolutely girlish sigh. It was rugged and strong and well defined, quite like the covers of my mother's paperback romance novels, and quite unlike Jarad Frampton, III, M.D. The little bit of *him* I'd seen exposed was soft, and white and flabby. It was hard to be stirred by such a future (assuming I still had a future with him since I hadn't heard a word from him since I'd sent that wire.) "Yes, I muttered, "I'm coming."

The corridor that ran from the back door to the stairs was a mess. The water might have been six inches deep in parts, confirming a long held suspicion of mind that the ground had settled since construction and left the floor slightly uneven. A mop was useless in such circumstances, so I went to the cupboard behind surgery and got the wide sidewalk broom Piers uses to sweep the flagstone of the courtyard in front, and literally swept a great portion of the water back out under the doorsill. Then we stopped up the space with two dozen of the green surgery towels, forcing them as far under the door as possible to keep them in place.

When the task was completed, Piers dropped to the floor, his arms wrapped around his knees, and rested his head against the wall, the picture of defeat. "Now I know why everyone else on this island builds their houses on stilts," he muttered. "I thought I knew more about foundations and drainage, coming from Holland. These so-called primitives knew better all along." He wiped water from his face with the back of his hand. "They're probably getting a good laugh from me right now."

I propped the broom in a corner and dragged a chair to the kitchen door. "I don't think they're giving you too much thought right now," I answered as another gust of wind slammed against the back door.

He shot me another undefinable look. "Sister," he said, gravely, "I would not think it cowardly if, right now, you missed your mother."

I slumped in my chair guiltily. "I confess that I don't."

"Well," Piers struggled to his feet, "I miss mine."

"Where is your mother?" I asked, following him back to the front room. "Is she still living?"

Piers shook his head. He was looking at a photograph of a white haired woman in a practical blue house dress. "She died while I was in medical school. It's sad, really, but at the time, I thought her frail and useless and a bit silly. However, looking back, I realize she was a wealth of reason and information about a time I never knew. She was a fountain of love and affection and self-affirmation that I shrugged off as unnecessary. She was long suffering and kind and 'specially gifted to be blind to the less savory things of life. I remember as a teen and young adult I thought of her as naïve and foolish, but I suppose what she was in reality was a marvelous blend of wisdom and innocence." He looked up and saw tears in my eyes. "What's this, Sister? What's wrong?"

"Now I *do* miss my mother," I wept, brushing at the tears with fingertips. "That's exactly how I feel about her…and, I suppose that's exactly how she is."

He turned away from the wall of photographs. "What she is, right now I imagine, is very worried about her daughter." He cocked his head, listening to the wind. "I wonder if we can get over to the Mission and put a call through to tell her you're all right."

I brushed the last of the tears away, "No, I'll wait until this passes and then just write her a note. She'll be all right." I followed him back to the stove. "If I know her, she's not even aware that there's anything happening in this part-" At the earsplitting crash, I jumped, throwing myself into Pier's arms. "What was that?"

His arms came around me and held me tight. "I think," he said, grimly, "that was the last window upstairs.

At first, all I could think about was the possibility that the house could come crashing down around us. Then, as I realized that wasn't going to happen, I thought how warm and smooth his skin was, how strong his heart sounded, how deep his voice was, how soothing his caress was. Finally, reluctantly, I realized I had no business lingering in his embrace and began to ease away.

"It's all right, Sister," he murmured, still holding me. "It's not cowardly to want to be comforted in situations like this, either."

"No, I'd better not," I managed to keep my voice even as I pulled free and dropped onto the ottoman before the stove. "The way I feel right now, if I started holding on, I might not ever let go."

"Well, well, well," Piers smiled as he bent to pick up the afghan, "so you're human after all." He let it drape around my shoulders. "I'll go see about the window."

"Be careful."

He flicked on the flashlight. "Don't worry, I will be."

The sun eventually came up in some parts of the China Sea, but over our little island, the sky was a dark, dull grey, and the wind continued to rage. I dozed off and on, curled up on a narrow settee and Piers sat on the floor beside me, trying to get his Mozart albums to play on my record player. Occasionally he would get up and try the radio in the corner, but the generator had given up the ghost and was not going to come back of its own volition.

Outside, the garden had been ripped up by the roots and the hundred old palms that stood behind the Mission were scattered, roots and all, across the courtyard and out into the road. Every sea facing window had been broken or completely blown out, allowing the wind to rush in, howling and whistling, throughout the tall, peach house.

Once in a while, I would shift uncomfortably on my make-do bed and Piers, with all the tenderness of a father, would bring the afghan up around my shoulders,

171

keeping me warm in that false chill. It was the false chill that must have reminded him of the brandy and he brought it back to the front room to take the bitter edge off the last of the coffee.

Disturbed by the wind racing over my head, I opened my eyes and saw Piers' profile as he sat on the floor, sipping spiked coffee and staring morosely into the past...or was it the future?

He must have sensed my eyes on him, for he turned and smiled a little, self-consciously. "Will you listen to that wind? It really does sound like the weeping of departed souls, doesn't it?"

I sat up, pulling the afghan around me, close. "You looked so sad, just now. Were you thinking about her departed soul?"

He turned again, trying to freeze me with a black ice glare, but I didn't back down. He took a long drink of cold coffee. "You do love to poke and pry, don't you, Sister?"

I shrugged. "Maybe I should have become a doctor...Doctor."

He emptied his cup and stared down into the emptiness. "As a matter of fact, I was not thinking about her. I seldom do, anymore. What I think about is what it is like without her."

I edged closer to him and asked quietly," What is it like without her?"

He sighed, deeply. "Lonely."

Oh, Piers, I thought sadly, my heart clenching in pain for him. *You don't have to be lonely*, I wanted to tell him, but I stayed silent.

"Now, you see what this kind of weather does to me?" He stood up and collected his cup. "It's a good thing you're going back in a few weeks," he said, not looking at me. "A girl as pretty and lively and compassionate as you shouldn't be cooped up on this island with a couple of baseball loving priests and a melancholy, widowed doctor."

I felt tears sting my eyes, not for his rebuke but for the painful image of a melancholy widowed doctor. "What will you do when I'm gone?" I asked, hoping he wouldn't hear the tears in my voice.

He turned off the little record player. "I'm going to request another assistant and hope the next one I get is a quiet living spinster who doesn't mind such an isolated life."

"I don't mind the isolated life," I protested.

"Now, do not start feeling sorry for me and think you can talk me into letting you stay." He shook a finger at me, reproachfully. "You're going back at first chance, Nurse

West, and that's the end of the discussion."
He turned on his heel and left me.

I groaned in frustration. "I'm getting
awfully tired of the way he walks out on
every argument," I told the empty room, and
the howling wind. I pushed the afghan away
and ran down the hall. "Hey!" I called. The
kitchen was empty. The bathroom was
empty except for the disaster of broken glass
and bits of vegetation. I came back to the
stairs and looked up, uncertainly, seeing the
glass shards that quivered tremulously in the
window casings. I really didn't want to
climb those stairs, even to find the doctor, but
I wanted the issue settled once and for all.
Fortunately, as I put a foot on the first step, I
heard a noise coming from surgery. I went
back down the hall and pushed open the door.
"Now, listen here Doctor-"

He was in the office, halfway into a fresh
pair of surgical greens.

"Oh." I backed up and would have
backed out, but I wasn't going to back down.
"Don't you like me, Dr. von Hollow?" I
demanded through the partially open door.

"Of course." His answer was muffled by
the shirt he was pulling over his head. "What
would make you ask a silly question like
that?" He tugged the door open and looked

down at me. "Have I ever given any indication that I don't like you?"

"Yes," I answered frankly. "All the time. Just now, for example." I flicked a hand toward the room across the hall. "You can't wait to get rid of me. I didn't expect to become your best friend, but I thought I had at least pulled my own weight as a nurse."

"Now *you* listen." He picked up his pajama pants from the pile he left on the floor and stuffed them into the bag for soiled laundry. "There's no denying that you're on your way to becoming an outstanding nurse. There is also no denying that you are young and extremely attractive, and every time I look at you I want to-" he stopped speaking and started to move.

For a moment I thought he was going to walk out on me once again and I began maneuvering myself to block him, but he stopped in front of me and very, very deliberately put a hand beneath my 'lemon drop' hair. He pulled me close to him and kissed me, deftly, deeply, determinedly. When he released me, we both seemed to have trouble breathing. "I shouldn't have done that," he said quietly and then he did walk out.

I didn't follow.

As I stood there, reeling, trying to reassure myself that what I thought had happened had happened, and that my prayers had been answered, there was a terrific pounding on the outer surgery door. Piers heard it, too, and was on my heels as I raced to open the door.

It was Fr. Richard and he was soaking wet and struggling for breath. "The temple in the village," he gasped, leaning against the door frame even as Piers and I tried to pull him inside. "It collapsed. Thirty, maybe forty people inside."

Piers released his friend. "I'll get my bag."

I brought Fr. Richard into the waiting room and into a chair. "I'm going, too," I announced.

"No, Heidi!" both men chorused and then exchanged glances that would have to be sorted out later. "It's too dangerous," Fr. Richard insisted. "The wind is almost impossible for me to pass through. You'll be blown away."

"I can handle myself," I argued. "Let me change my-"

Piers caught my arm, roughly. "No, Heidi, I won't let you go. If anything happened to you I'd never forgive myself." He looked at the priest. "Richard, take her to the Mission."

"But-" I began.

"And if you have to, chain her to something." Piers was out the door and running into the wind.

Chapter Eleven
The Declaration

"Well, you are without a doubt the prettiest priest I've ever seen," Fr. Richard announced, bringing tea from a pot on the old, blackened stove.

"Fr. Richard!" I scolded, nervously rolling the sleeves of the long brown habit the priests had provided for me. I was sure there was some Holy Rule about a woman wearing a priest's robe and I was just begging to be struck by lightning or written down in some book recording mortal sins. "You aren't allowed to say things like that."

"Sure we are," he countered, returning with a rough, crockery bowl of sugar. "Beauty is one of God's many gifts. We would be ungrateful if we didn't appreciate it." He handed me a spoon. "Of course, appreciation, as in all things, must be done with moderation." He sank down on the long, narrow bench across the refectory table from me.

"I don't know." I hunched into the garment, patched and heavy but soft from years of laundering and wear. "Everything about this would make the sisters at Santa Theresa faint."

"Don't you believe it," he retorted stirring his tea loudly. "Every nun I've ever known has been as practical as she was compassionate. You don't stay in this service without having the rough edges knocked off early on."

"Like being a nurse, I suppose." I spooned a little sugar into my own cup.

"Exactly. Little by little the textbooks fade and real life becomes your instructor."

"Well, that's certainly true." A gust of wind rattled the shutters behind me and I shuddered and glanced over my shoulder. "Someone should have gone with him."

"He wouldn't have let me," Fr. Richard assured me. "Don't worry. Piers knows this island as well as you and I. Well," he grinned, "Better than you do."

Blushing, I stared into my tea. Fr. Richard had made it too strong for my tastes, but after the drenching I'd received in the frantic dash to get to the shelter of the Mission, I was grateful for it. "Why does he dislike me so much?"

"Dislike you?" Fr. Richard arched a brow. "That's not the word I would use."

"All right, maybe that's a little strong, but in his own words he can't wait for me to go home."

"Heidi, it's for your own good," the priest answered plainly. "This is no place for a pretty young girl."

"That's just what he said." I took a drink and made a face. "Honestly, I'm hardly some wild party girl, missing the dances and parties."

"It's not just that. Heidi, these are dangerous times. There is political unrest in the bigger cities already. Sooner or later it is going to spill over to the outlying areas, such as our village." He lowered his voice, leaning across the wooden table to make sure than only she heard his words. "Sukarno wants total control - a dictatorship - and he is trying to remove any Western influence that might oppose him. Consequently he's reviving a strong anti-Dutch sentiment. I fear for Piers, but he has always ignored me. Well, he can't ignore the potential danger to you just being associated with him."

"What about me? Don't my feelings matter?"

Fr. Richard rested his chin on his fist and looked at me. "Just what are your feelings?"

I was startled by the directness of his question. "What do you think this is? A confessional?"

He shrugged those broad shoulders. "If you like. Might be good for the soul."

"My soul is fine, thank you." I took another sip of tea, feeling his eyes boring into me. "My feelings are nothing special. I like it here." I felt ready to meet his gaze and looked up. "I like the feeling of seeing the job through. I don't like being chased off as if I were just a pesky child."

"Oh, so it's your ego that got bruised." Fr. Richard dismissed it with the tone of his voice. "I was starting to think something else was involved."

"What are you talking about?" I tried to laugh airily. It wasn't even remotely convincing.

"I'm talking about the way you looked last night when you realized he was trying to cross in the middle of a storm. The way you looked when he said he was going out to the village this morning. The way you looked-"

"Oh, so it's my eyes that are involved," I retorted, mimicking his earlier observation.

"No, Sister Lemon Drop, I think it's something about twelve inches lower."

I knew what he meant and I knew I was blushing at the suggestion. "Oh, that," I said, trying again to laugh. "Every nurse gets a crush on her doctor. It's the most common thing in the world."

"Of course it is," Fr. Richard agreed, doubtfully.

"You should know…it's the central plot in a dozen of those soap operas you like on the radio."

Fr. Richard sat back, hands flat on the table, frowning at me as if disappointed.

I continued to stir my tea and a heavy silence fell between us. Fr. Richard listened to the wind and I listened to the echo of all the words Piers and I had exchanged through the night. Suddenly, I sat up straight and whispered, "A melancholy widower."

Fr. Richard, who had been lulled almost into a stupor, blinked at me. "What?"

"I said a melancholy – Fr. Richard," I pinned a look on him. "What happened to his wife?"

"Now you're getting a little personal," the priest said in disapproval. "If he wanted you to know-"

"He told me," I insisted impatiently, "but, I wasn't paying attention. Is he divorced or not?"

"Piers? I don't *think* so," Fr. Richard said with a harsh laugh that was clearly meant to convey grim irony rather than humor.

I waited.

"His wife died last year, just before he came to us. In fact," he lowered his voice again, "I think that's why he came."

I lowered my voice, too. "What happened to her?"

Fr. Richard shook his head.

"Did he tell you in confession?" I demanded.

"No, of course not. Piers isn't of the Church. He doesn't believe in-"

"Then you're under no obligation not to tell me." I pounded my fist on the table for emphasis.

Fr. Richard's brows rose at my response. Mine did, too...internally. He sat back and considered it. I think he wanted to tell me all along, but wanted to be able to tell Piers I forced it from him. "You might have read about some terrible flooding in Amsterdam last year."

I nodded. I hadn't heard, but it would save time if I pretended I had.

"She and the children were trying to get across the channel to the main road out of town-"

"The children?" I repeated, feeling a growing ache inside. "He has children?"

Fr. Richard shook his head sadly. "They had two sons, but the family was trapped on a bridge when a surge of water came up the channel and they were swept away."

"Oh, no!" I pressed a fist to my mouth to keep from screaming. "Oh, that poor, poor man."

"Yes. Evidently she was from the farm country, and had never experienced flooding there at the sea's edge. She didn't know it was safer to stay upstairs in the house than to try and cross the channel." He leaned across the table and patted my hand. "Don't let on that you know. He doesn't want anyone to know. It's his cross to bear, he says, and he doesn't want anyone to have to share the load."

"How do you know about it?" I was surprised to hear my voice, it was weak and trembling.

He shrugged. "Someone introduced him to *tuak* one night. Like you, he got a little intoxicated and it all spilled out, complete with tears. After that, he took out every drop of alcohol in the whole place so he would never, ever tell the story again. If it were up to him, I doubt there would be rubbing alcohol in his office."

I didn't say anything. I didn't even nod to indicate my comprehension, but inside I was sobbing, 'That poor, poor man.'

When the storm went, it went completely. One moment the sky was black and the wind was raging and the next moment a brilliant red and purple sunset was settling over the horizon and the air was clean and dry and almost cool.

I went back to the tall, peach house, then, still in my borrowed habit, and surveyed the wreckage. All of the windows that faced the sea were gone. There were watermarks as high as two feet in the hall and around the kitchen walls. The little shelf of curios in the downstairs lavatory had fallen and cracked the back of the commode but, curiously, none of the little knick knacks were broken. A shelf of cups and saucers in the kitchen wasn't so lucky. The seat cushions of the kitchen chairs were soaked and ruined and the pretty blue curtains in the kitchen window had been shredded by wind and broken glass.

There was sand and debris in the kitchen, the lav, the hall and even the upstairs landing. The bedrooms seemed to have survived with only some paint damage and the front room seem to have come through completely unscathed. The only sign in the surgery that there had even been a storm was the supine figure on the examining table, bearded, bloodied and begrimed.

I saw him and my heart broke. I wanted to comfort him but I knew he would not welcome my comfort. He had lost those things most precious to him. No wonder he had come to this isolated island. He didn't want anyone who reminded him of youth and love and gaiety. *He's right,* I thought, watching him sleep, *I should leave as soon as possible.*

As I turned to leave, he lifted his head. "Heidi?"

I looked at him. "Sorry, I didn't mean to wake you."

"That's all right." He swung his legs around to sit up at the edge of the exam table, and rubbed his eyes. Then, lifting his head, he listened. "It's over."

I nodded. "About an hour ago. Are you all right? You have blood all over you."

He looked down at his greens. "There was a lot of blood but nothing too serious, thank God. No fatalities. Not even major casualties. It seems several men had been drinking when the storm moved inland and they took shelter in the temple." He managed a weak smile. "I suppose if one is in the condition those men were in, having a bamboo hut fall down around one is not a momentous occasion." He eased himself to the floor. "I'm empty. Is there anything salvageable in the kitchen?"

"It's a mess," I agreed, "but I'm sure we can manage something."

"What a strange smile, Heidi," he observed. So sad. Why so sad?"

I shook my head and backed a step or toward the door. "I'm not sad, just tired."

"Don't like to me while you're dressed up like a priest. It's…It's obscene."

I drew a deep, shaky breath. "I guess I was forced to decide that you're right. I should go home. As soon as possible."

He raised a brow but said nothing.

"I'm going upstairs and change clothes if I can. You're right. Doing anything dressed like a priest seems a little obscene." That wasn't true. I just wanted to get away from him before I burst into tears.

Piers rubbed his chin. "Me, too." He followed me to the door. "Tell me, Sister, while you're still dressed as a priest, is this amazing change of heart because I kissed you?"

Yes! I nearly screamed, but with effort I gave him a silent, haughty smile. "Is that what you think? I can stand up to a monsoon but a little kiss will send me running? You must think I'm an absolutely baby."

"A baby? No, that is *not* what I think." He caught my shoulder. "And I also do not think that kiss scared you. I think it was that kiss meant that scared you."

"M-meant?" I stammered as he swung me around to face him, and forced me against the water stained wall. "What could a kiss mean?" Once again, I tried the pathetic little laugh that was so useless with Fr. Richard. "It means you find me attractive, that's all."

"Hardly." He kissed me again, roughly. "It means I find you..." he struggled for words and when he found none he released me and backed away. "Go upstairs and change, Sister. We have a lot to do today."

I didn't opt for a dignified, nonchalant exit. I ran. I ran as if I expected him to chase me up the stairs and show me exactly what that kiss meant.

I stayed upstairs, too. At first, I convinced myself that I had a lot to do. I washed my hair and changed my clothes. I changed several times because I suddenly didn't feel comfortable in my usual shortened shorts and sleeveless shirts, and ended up in a cotton turtleneck and long jeans. I wrote a letter to my mother, telling her in great detail about the monsoon and that I would be home soon. I made my bed. I straightened my things. I paced. I put all my books and music in the bottom of my case as if I expected to leave that night. I packed my clothes. I paced some more. I sat on the bed and stared into space, unwilling to think about Piers, because if I did, I'd go downstairs and let him kiss me again, and again, and...

"Are you coming down, or not? I've got a full surgery all of a sudden, and I need a nurse." Piers was at the door, clean shaven, neatly combed, in fresh greens. He sent his eyes over my ensemble and scowled. "Get a move on," he snapped.

I moved. I was glad there was going to be a surgery because that would delay my need to be alone with him. Maybe I could come right back upstairs and hide from him until he was ready to take me back to Java. Feeling safer in my cotton uniform and starched cap, I came back downstairs.

We worked by candle and flashlight, stitching up a cut here, disinfecting an abrasion there, setting a couple of broken bones, administering tetanus shots and antibiotics. I threw myself into the work, forbidding myself to dwell on how much I would miss it: the people, the place, the independence, the doctor.

Finally, the last of the storm's victims were treated and gone and I was left alone with Piers.

He came into the office as I filed away charts. He stood in the door a long time, watching me. I felt his presence by refused to turn and look at him until he spoke to me, very softly. "Do you really want to go?" he asked me.

I nodded jerkily. "I think it's best."

He shook his head behind me. I could feel it. "I didn't think Dr. Frampton meant that much to you."

I finally whirled around, moth open in surprise. "What does Jarad have to do with this?"

"Everything." He shrugged. "You're a girl of honor, Heidi. No one could ever doubt that. You must feel as if you've betrayed his trust by letting me kiss you, enjoying that I did."

"'Enjoying?'" I repeated, indignantly. "What makes you think I enjoyed it?"

He shrugged again, moving closer. "Shall I prove it?"

I backed up against the filing cabinet. "No."

He backed up a step. "Then you do feel as if you betrayed him."

"No." I looked at the file in my hands. "Jarad doesn't have anything to do with this. I did enjoy kissing you. I wanted you to kiss me again, but you can't," I added when he

190

started to move closer again. "I'm old fashioned. There. You know the worst about me. I can't fall into bed with you just because I like the way you kiss me, but I know if I stayed here I would."

He reached out and took the file from me and opened it, studying it carefully. "Are you trying to tell me you don't have casual affairs?" he said as if commenting on some entry I had made in the file. "Good Heavens, Heidi, don't you think I know that?" He raised his eyes to mine. "I've known that since I first met you. That's been the problem all along."

He tossed the file on the desk top, turning his back to me. "If you were the kind of girl a man could use for a casual affair, we would have started one right after you got here, and it would have been no hardship for me." He shot a glance over his shoulder that started at my knees and slid up to my eyes. "But, you're not the kind of girl man could *use* for anything. You tend to bring out the Boy Scout in a man. I found that frustrating."

I stood there, wondering if I was supposed to apologize, but he went on. "Then I noticed that I liked you. I liked your sense of humor and your sense of practicality. I liked you stubborn determination and your desire to do things right. I liked the way your eyes sparkle when you laugh. I liked the compassion that puts silver lights in your eyes when something makes you sad." He looked at his hands. "You see, Heidi, I started letting myself care about you. Yesterday I wanted you to go home for your sake. This morning I wanted you to go home for mine. And now…" He shrugged. "Now, I can't let you go home." He twisted away. "No, I'm not asking you to stay. I know you hate the heat and the isolation and the storms. I know there's danger here for you with the growing anti-Western attitudes in this country. I couldn't make you stay for all that. I couldn't let you be endangered, but…I'll tell you, Heidi," he bit down on his lip as if to steady it, "putting you on a plane back to the United States is going to be the second hardest thing I've ever done."

I was shaking. I couldn't think about what I should do or say. I couldn't think about the suggestion of tears in his eyes or in the words he had spoken. I only knew that I was shaking. Someone was taking my life and tipping upside down, rearranging everything, changing it forever. Maybe it was changing for the better but it was harder, too. "Yes," I said finally. "I hate the heat and the storms and maybe, sometimes, the isolation, but it doesn't matter because I love you."

It took him a long time to react and at first I thought his reaction was anger; he turned toward me so slowly, his brows drawn together in a painfully familiar scowl. "What," he demanded raggedly, "did you say?"

"I said I love you." I spoke with more conviction this time. "I know you won't ever let yourself love anyone again. I understand that. I know what all I have to offer is companionship and-and sex." I lowered my eyes, blushing. "But, if that's all you want, why not take it when it's offered willingly?"

He didn't pull me into his arms and smother me with kisses the way the men always did in my mother's romance novels. He didn't sweep me into his arms and carry me upstairs to bed. He didn't crush me against his chest and vow to love me for eternity. He caught both my shoulders and shook me, almost furiously. "Shame on you, Heidi West. Shame on you."

Now the tears did come. "I don't understand," I sobbed. "What do you want?"

"It's not what I want. It's what you want. You've compromised everything in your life to satisfy others. It's time to draw a line, and look after your own need. I don't want an affair because you're willing to give in once again. I don't want you in my bed believing that I'll get bored and send you home. I want commitment, Heidi. I believe in it. I want you to give me the same commitment you've given to nursing, but not because I'm asking you to but because you love me. Not because your mother, or Richard or me or anyone else in the world tells you to do it. Do it because you think it's the right thing for you to do. What's right for you, Heidi West? What's right for you?"

I lifted my eyes and he looked so fierce I wanted to look away immediately, but I faced him steadfastly. "You," I said firmly. "You're what's right for me. I want to stay here and help you rebuild this house so it won't blow down next year. I want to help you build your practice – our practice. I want to face whatever the future holds for us – no matter what's happening in Java. I want to be so busy, so involved that I don't have time to get bored. I want you to teach me so you'll never get bored. That's what is right for me, Piers von Hollow. Loving you is what's right for me."

He did kiss me then. It was a different kiss, a sweet kiss that grew demanding yet remained controlled. I felt him tremble a little as he wound his arms around me, and then he pushed himself away. "What's right for you this moment, however, is to move over to the Mission."

"The Mission?" My soaring heart was dashed to the ground. "But, why?"

"Because I won't marry you until your mother can be here to see you wed, and I'll go crazy having you in this house until I can marry you." He kissed me again, quickly, as if sealing the deal. "Go pack your things, Sister." He started for the surgery door. "I'm going to go over and make arrangements for you, and if I can manage, get your mother on the first place out here. What are you staring at?"

"Marry?" I repeated. I didn't remember any part of the discussion that included marriage. I'd made my offer without any demands for marriage and I hadn't expected any offers, either. "You want to marry me?"

"Yes. Yes, damn it, I want to wake up every morning and see that lemon drop hair on the other pillow of my bed, and that won't happen unless I marry you." He reached for my chin and tilted it up until I had to meet his eyes. "It will be for keeps, Heidi, so think it over carefully before you say yes. Oh." He glanced away, swallowed hard and looked back at me. "Lest you get any ideas that the previous Mrs. von Hollow set a precedent, she didn't leave me in the literal sense. She died."

I pulled back just enough that his fingers slipped away from my face. "I know."

His skin darkened. "Richard. I might have known. It's frightening to think that the man actually hears confession. He cannot keep a secret."

"It wasn't his fault," I explained quickly. "I practically tortured him to get the story. I just wanted to understand…" how could I tell him I wanted to understand why he didn't seem to be interested in me? "I just wanted to understand, that's all. I didn't realize, until he told me, just how deeply I'd been prying into your pain. I'm sorry."

Piers struggled with it for a moment. "It's all right. You should know, really. I wouldn't want you always wondering where she was and if she was suddenly going to pop back into my life. She's still with me, here." He pressed a fist to his chest. "She always will be, but there's plenty of room for you, as well." He opened his hand and let his fingers brush my hair back from my face. "You never responded to my statement. How do you feel about this idea of mine, this idea of getting married?"

I realized I had finally stopped shaking. My heart had slipped back into place and the ache I felt was that of a joy that couldn't be contained or expressed. "I feel just fine about it," I answered breathlessly. "Just fine.

The end

Postscript:

We didn't stay in Indonesia forever, as we had planned. Piers sent me back to the big peach house in Holland when our first child was due, and he came back the following year, 1964.

Martial law, which had managed to keep friction between various political factions at a minimum since 1957, was rescinded, and a full scale, anti-Western, anti-democracy campaign began. Pier's license to practice medicine in Java was revoked, and our house on the beach was commandeered. Piers resisted as long as he could; unmanageable inflation and failing infrastructure left many villages and towns without medical care.

We stayed in Amsterdam until our third child was old enough to walk, and then we left Holland to practice medicine in Botswana, but we carried the memories of the people, the beautiful country, the colorful history and rich culture of Indonesia with us wherever we went.

Perle Butcher-Lyon is from a long line of historical observers. Her favorite occupation as a child was listening to the stories of her parents, grandparents and great grandparents, about when they were growing up. Her goal was to create romantic ephemera of a period that represented the best and the worst of humanity.

If you enjoyed *The Dutch Doctor*, if you have questions or constructive comments, you may contact her at PerleB@inknbeans.com and look for her other book *The Wreck Of the Sidonie Stone*, also available at fine booksellers and at

Fresh Books Brewed Daily

www.ingramcontent.com/pod-product-compliance
Lightning Source LLC
Chambersburg PA
CBHW070840120626
46556CB00002B/821